Poison Among Us

Exposing the Reasons Women Hurt Women

By

Deborah Johnson Spence, Ph.D.

Poison Among Us: Exposing the Reasons Women Hurt Women

Published by G Publishing LLC, 800.478.2691,
www.gpublishingsuccess.com

In association with
Your Concerns, Inc
P. O. Box 23357
Detroit, MI 48223
www.yourconcernscounseling.com
prayerboard@msn.com

Printed in the USA.

Library of Congress
Cataloging-in-Publication Data
        Spence, Deborah Ph.D.
        Fiction: Contemporary Woman
        Religion: Christian Life-Women's Issues
        Psychology: Interpersonal Relations

Library of Congress Control Number: 2008901412
ISBN   13: 978-0-9815851-0-9
          10: 0-9815851-0-8

The author is available for counseling, coaching, workshops, lectures and
other speaking engagements.
Contact Dr. Deborah Spence at prayerboard@msn.com .

Book edited by Eugene Seals EugeSeals@yahoo.com
Cover designed by Jackie Baptist

The scenarios in this novel are based on reality. The story line and the
characters are fictional and are not intended to represent any real persons,
living or dead. Any parallels to any real persons are purely coincidental.

Foreword

"I am because we are; we are because I am." This African proverb has been my mantra for most of my adult life. It has been reinforced on my spiritual journey and facilitates my connections between the shoulders I stand on and those who will stand on mine.

Yet, despite a strong legacy as a womanist, I'm bewildered by the destructive interactions between women--mothers and daughters, biological sisters, family members, sisters in Christ, college roommates, female colleagues in the workplace or in advocacy organizations, sorority sisters, and neighbors.

I regularly ask myself, "WHY do we perpetuate the predictably divisive behaviors regardless of our geography, culture, race, generation, religion, or socio-economic status? WHY can't we be happy for each other's successes and joys? WHY do we so quickly assume negative intent, enter into adversarial stances, and reject opportunities to seek understanding? Why do we not recognize the models we have inherited and how we transfer them to future generations?"

As I watch my seven granddaughters, I get excited about their girly innocence--the giggles, the sleepovers, the dress-up sessions, the care they give their dolls individually and collectively. But I worry about the world of womanhood they will inherit. I also feel tremors of guilt for any role I have played, wittingly or unwittingly, in sustaining the dysfunctional female persona that they may mirror.

Poison Among Us is the first contemporary glimmer of hope that will serve as a critical agent of change. The research and authentic case studies compiled and analyzed by Dr. Deborah Spence objectively begin awareness building concerning Woman-on-Woman Abuse. This first stage will result in the conversations and transparent dialogue required for women to acknowledge what has plagued our existence for centuries. I look forward to our individual and collective acceptance as well as the interventions which will lead to fulfilling God's promise for our potential.

Jacquelyn B. Gates,
President and CEO
SOARing, LLC

Dedication

To all the women who have ever suffered abuse from another woman.

Acknowledgments

It seems that no author has been more blessed with such a loyal circle of supporters as I. Consequently, while apologizing in advance for the risk of leaving some of them out, let me mention a few.

Ultimate acknowledgments go to God for gifting me for his purposes.

Next, I gratefully thank my husband, Roger, whose stupendous fortitude and indulgence are more than I could ever hope for.

To my adult children Justin, Carina, and Abe I say: Thoughts of you and your encouragement consistently make me smile.

Thanks to my insightful editor, Eugene Seals, who chivalrously and graciously shifted roles, learned to speak the language of Venus, and had the courage to tell me no far more times than I am accustomed. You, Gene, are a true GEM.

Thank you to Jackie Baptist, graphic artist, who has the patience of Job.

Thank you to my mother-friends Janet Nunley, Ora Galloway, Avis Cadogen, and Shirley Seals, who kept me grounded in the absence of my mother.

Thank you to my mentors Doris Gothard, Dr. Barbara Weems, and Dr. Elsie Jackson (my Dissertation Chair), whose characters, coupled with their achievements, have made them giants.

Because their levity kept me buoyant, I thank my fabulous friends and supporters Edwina Autrey, Dr. Helen Bryant, Dr. Gwendolyn Grady-Dansby, Dr. Wayne Darville, Dr. Audré

Dixon, Thora Greaves, Dr. Peggy Ncube, Bernadine Johnson, Cathryn Johnson, Emilie Johnson, Cheryl Steinman (Mary Kay™ National Sales Director), Allyson Lane Williams, and my prayer partner, Tim. Also, included as friends and supporters are the gorgeous models, who so eloquently represent the ages and ethnicities of women in this study: Candace Walls, Kimberly Donaldson, Mattie Hensley, and Michelle Henson.

I also thank the womanist Jacqui Gates, who is a true spiritual woman of valor.

To my sisters of the African Seventh-Day Adventist Church: You collectively demonstrate the love of Jesus and inclusion as best I have ever seen a group of women do. *Ngiyabonga. Baie dankie. Fofo. Ke a leboga. Asante. Zikomo. Tatenda. Webale. Neyanziza. Wakora.*

Last, but not least, I acknowledge the late Emma Wiggins Johnson, my mother and very best friend.

Contents

Chapter 1 – Dissonance

Contrary to widespread opinion in Christian circles, the Voices of Gabriel choir works hard to produce what appears to be effortless music. "No pain, no gain," they say.

For that reason, in the well-lit, but poorly acoustically endowed basement amphitheatre of the *Temple in the Sky*, we rehearsed a difficult passage for the third time, finally producing the elusive ephemeral chords, achieving the lingering dissonance, and evoking the wonderfully cathartic pathos which the composer intended.

Making contrasting chords sound angelic isn't easy, but Cindy, our fabulous director, has a gift of musical interpretation. The blend of what seemed to be conflicting notes was now performed perfectly. Cindy jumped, applauded, and shouted *Hallelujah*! to give vent to emotions of joy because we, her friends and mentees, had finally reached another milestone of musical excellence. Meanwhile, the typically straight-laced Bobby displayed an uncharacteristic, hard-to-elicit smile of approval as he swayed seemingly precariously from his perch at the Hammond console.

The musical segment had been truly angelic, full of pathos, unlike some of the members of the choir who shall remain nameless, at least for now, lest I get ahead of myself. What good is a yarn if you give it all away at the outset? [No fair peeking ahead to the end of the book, either. I'm watching you.]

Were it not for my new husband's twenty-five year attachment to this choir, I definitely would have been out of there. Despite their angelic sound, some of them [or some of us] had some real issues. Far be it from me to try to correct them all. But…if you will come a little closer, I may whisper something in your ear.

Listen. Pssst.… Many of us are seriously afflicted by that which is unseen, unrealized, and not understood, but painfully, obviously present. The downside is that we remain clueless to that fact. Well, that's enough for now. Let's get back to the choir.

The choir continued to sing as an older woman [mid-sixties was older to me] walked into the room. She tried not to draw attention to herself, but it was impossible not to be drawn to her. She tiptoed quietly, respectfully, as she made her way across the large rehearsal room toward the choir loft even while we were still busy imprinting the correct chords into our neural pathways.

There was something distinctive about her, adorned as she was with the grace of a swan, the countenance of a woman of great achievements, and the self-effacing meekness of a Japanese performing artist, a geisha. Curiously, there was something very familiar about this woman – something the two of us shared. This intrigued me! She reminded me of my future, but not exactly my future. It was as if we had entered a time warp and I was already well acquainted with Estelle. Kind of eerie, isn't it?

She alighted into an end chair with all the elegance of a monarch butterfly. Cindy stopped directing the choir long enough to ask her name.

"Estelle Devereaux," she replied, then quickly and humbly added, "I've been coming to this church a long time."

Cindy wasn't like many of the other women in the choir. She extended a genuine "Welcome!" and passed sheet music to Estelle.

Estelle wore a closely woven, salmon-colored, silk suit. Her shoes and matching handbag were taupe. You could almost miss the understated detail that went into their construction. Subtle elegance – just what I admire. Full, soft brown hair graced her shoulders tenderly and framed her reddish skin tone. Her Egyptian-like features were stunning, even behind the mask sculpted by decades of life.

Another thirty minutes passed, and the one and-one-half hour rehearsal ended. Estelle approached me and introduced herself, "Hello. I am Estelle Devereaux."

"Hi. I'm Beth Johnson. I noticed you when you came in. Welcome."

"Thank you," she smiled, adding, "I am not much of a singer, but I like music and I like choirs."

"You know, Estelle, I'm not much of a singer either."

As we exchanged pleasantries, I recognized it again. It was strong! I had a need to let her know I understood. It is strangely wonderful how birds of a feather recognize their own.

* * *

Two weeks later, hubby and I arrived early for worship. I loved the Lord and I loved being in His presence; but I dreaded going to the *Temple in the Sky*. It always reminded me of my own 'crucifixion' which had been a slow process of no less than two years. Even though my crucifixion is finally over, residuals remain, taking the form of social exclusion, condescending looks, and – worst of all – spiritual superiority of Amazon proportions.

I am not the only victim of this ancestral arrogance, proudly linked as it is to a historical icon I call The Mayflower. The Mayflower isn't a flower at all. It is, rather, a concept. The Mayflower is a term used to describe the dogmatic craft nurtured and preserved by generation after generation within the church that I affectionately refer to as the *Temple in the Sky*.

I cringe every time my brother-in-law tells The Mayflower story. It absolutely amazes me! How could he exult in such ridiculousness? After all, when the *Temple in the Sky*, or what he affectionately refers to as The Mayflower, began; he wasn't even a twinkle in his parents' eyes. Yet, he rears back with his thumbs in his proverbial suspenders and delightfully boasts that the members with influence are related to him and are directly linked to the church's origin.

He never fails to follow with such biologically incorrect phrases as "So-and-so was born in the church." Trust me. I can not imagine one woman who went through the pangs of childbirth on one of the hard pews in the tastefully appointed sanctuary. I always hold my peace because, technically speaking, I suppose, if we are Christians, we are born in the church.

My impressions of The Mayflower were quite different, as seen through the eyes of my mother. She had boarded The Mayflower while still a young girl in the company of her mother (my grandmother) and eight siblings.

Grandma Maxie was happy serving the Lord and praising His holy name anywhere and everywhere. Whether a peach in her Georgia home town or an import in the *Temple in the Sky*, she was one of the rare breed that loves the Lord no matter what.

Grandma Maxie was a little taller than the average woman, with wavy, jet black hair complemented by smooth, dark skin. I imagine that her hue may have changed as a result of years of suffering from anoxia, secondary to chronic asthma. Her body wasn't assimilating enough oxygen, leaving her weak, often struggling to breathe. Sick or not, there was no missing her strong personality. Her unique features were keen. Like Momma's. Like Estelle's, the new woman in the basement.

Momma had an interesting appearance. She was short and had smooth skin the shade of light caramel milk. Her frame was petite, but her breasts were large. She had supple, sandy brown hair and green eyes with traces of hazel and grey. She was soft spoken and was often found in the company of her sisters because other girls often teased her about her cat-eyes.

Yet, seventy-six years after Grandma first visited this church, I sat in the same craft, namely the *Temple in the Sky*, receiving a healthy dose of what I perceived as the same estrangement and condescending looks as I am sure my mother had been accustomed to. But this time, there really was a reason for the disdain.

All the cliques had identified an eligible candidate for Robert's (my new husband) affection. Shhh! The question is whether these infatuations developed before or after his former wife died from breast cancer.

Pssst. I was the dark horse candidate who from out of nowhere began visiting the *Temple in the Sky.* But, there I go, getting ahead of myself again. Where were we? Ah, yes! In church.

At the end of the service, Estelle, the lady from the basement went down to the front of the church in a come-to-Jesus way. Only she gave a testimony. She said that she had been diagnosed with a cancerous liver tumor, but that the tumor was now gone. *Amen* was the congregation's enthusiastic response! *Amen!*

After church, Robert and I sat down for our customary Sabbath meal. We discussed inviting others to join us the following week. For me the list of possibilities was short. It was one thing to go to a stuffy church where members resented me. It was another matter to bring the pythons home. However, to gain friends one must show oneself friendly.

[This display of friendliness is what I had done years ago when with a horrific tooth pain I found myself in Dr. Light's chair. She had that certain elegant persona, also, but was unaffected by it. She was planning a party, so I offered to cater a few *hors d'eouvres* and fruit trays free of charge, if she would buy the ingredients. She did, and we hit it off. Little did I know that she would introduce me to my future husband, Robert.]

* * *

The next Sabbath came. At church, I scouted the audience and foyer for individuals to invite home for dinner. I spotted Murray, whose family was away on vacation. We had sort of grown up together. He accepted my invitation with gratitude. He had grown tired of his own cooking. He, my husband, our two children, and I would make five. Now, we needed three more for a full table.

I noticed a seemingly harmless couple. The wife had been my roommate in boarding school, and the husband had transferred in from another denomination. Great! They would make six and seven. I needed one last person. Of course! Silly me. Why not ask the Lady in the basement? ... She accepted graciously! Then, fine, next Sabbath we would have a dinner party.

Friday came too soon. Unfortunately, my sister Jennifer and I had both waited until the last minute to gather groceries. We left the market waving at each other, and I headed home.

It was two in the afternoon when the kitchen door flung open, hitting the wall behind it with a bang. As I rushed in, I struggled to carry four full plastic bags which stressed both my right leg and shoulder under the burden of their weight. One bag, a little too full of milk and canned goods, stretched as the handle expanded until it scraped the floor.

It was obvious that I was not to place the groceries on the counter top successfully when several cans of tomato sauce spilled out of the bag and rolled across the white tiled floor. Dropping to my knees, I released the bags and chased the rolling cans. Before I stood to my feet, I cleared my vision by restraining a couple of brown twists that had fallen into my eyes and pulling them behind my ear.

Oops. my eyes gazed at the clock on the microwave. I must hurry! I quickly organized the cans on the counter and began my famous sprint down the preparatory stretch.

I pulled out the fresh chicken breasts, spices, and other groceries as I simultaneously searched the recipe cards neatly cataloged in the can covered with bright flowers like those found in meadows. Working quickly is something I do well. Like Momma, I loved laughing and chatting with Jennifer.

There! In short order, dinner was finished. The chicken cacciatore smelled divine. The bread was baked. The green bean almondine was left a bit undercooked, so it could stand reheating tomorrow when the guests arrived. The kitchen, like the rest of the house, was clean; and I could now take care of my special touches before the Sabbath.

So I set the table with oversized plates that were dramatically sunken in the center. Along the edge of the plates were splashes of bright reds, oranges, and purples, speckled with throws of gold. The napkins were bright red and fanned out of the top and the bottom of winding gold napkin rings. The long stem glasses were more art deco, floating out to the painted gold scalloped rims.

Hidden behind each large glass was a smaller clone of the large glass. The larger was for water; the smaller for a family tradition, sparkling grape juice, which tastes like non-alcoholic champagne! Six scented, ball shaped candles resembling sand sculptures topped each candle holder. The center of the table exploded with exotic flowers. Of all the flowers, my personal favorites were the birds of paradise.

To preserve the beautifully adorned dining room table, the family ate a simple supper in the nook: home-made potato soup and fresh corn bread. Just as the sun was setting, we talked about how we were happy that the week was finally at an end and shared personal testimonies. After the testimonies, Robert offered prayer, thanking God for our individual blessings and for blessing us as a family. We studied tomorrow's lesson study and relaxed before going to bed.

In the morning, the old ladies marveled at Robert's antics and blushed from the candor of his lesson study questions. He was introverted by nature, but something magical happened when he had an audience. I shook my head at him and softly muttered, "Unm, unm, unm." He smiled a private smile.

Service was even better than usual. It was always that way when the pastor bore a burden. Surely, he must have been tried in some kind of fire the first six days of the week, because the gold was blatantly evident. His sermon brought down the roof and even stirred the few women who were of second generation Mayflower lineage, were self-declared matriarchal antiques void of any sort of emotion. Their male counterparts had no such reaction, for the sermon was evidence that their scheme to remove the pastor was working. I scanned the audience for the queen bee who was behind most of the dissension in the church. There she sat, feigning blamelessness, yet guilty as sin.

Cindy jumped up at the appeal and directed the choir to sing one of those come-to-Jesus Songs. Boy, did they sing out! *Amens*! Came from all quarters. The saints *sho nuff* had *chirch* that morning!

We didn't stay to shake hands and fellowship with folks because we were expecting guests. When we got home, I placed some sparkling red grape juice in an ice bucket on the diminutive, crescent shaped bar. Another bottle of room temperature red grape juice was strategically placed next to the chilling bottle, so that guests could have their preference.

While the food warmed, I made the salads. The salads were works of art, if I do say so myself. First, the red leaf lettuce made an outward presentation as it lay on the outer edge of the salad plate. I then followed by placing the green bib lettuce as an inward ring and center. Inside the inward ring and center of bib lettuce, I laid two ribbed cucumber slices, a sprinkle of dried cherries and walnuts, three rings of red onions, and mandarin oranges arranged in the shape of a flower, accompanied by a small bright yellow edible flower. Delicately delightful! When we escorted our guests into the dining room, everything was perfect.

Dinner was as tasty as it was lovely. After a delicious repast and a time of socializing, most of our guests began leaving; but Estelle was just warming up. She followed me to the kitchen and begged to help. This was her first time in our home and my rule was to refuse help from first-time guests. But there was something in her eyes, a cry and a plea bordering on despair. I accepted her offer.

Being in the kitchen with Estelle reminded me of working in the kitchen with my mother. She was pleasantly charming and a hard worker, too. We rinsed the dishes and organized them so that washing would be easier later. After the kitchen was presentable, we went into the living room where we sank into an oversized high-back Queen Anne sofa filled with down.

She began telling me about her life. "Beth, I want to thank you for inviting me to dinner. That was a kind thing for you to do."

"My pleasure! Estelle. We haven't had the pleasure of getting to know each other yet. Have we?"

"Not at all," replied Estelle. "I've felt comfortable around you ever since that day in the basement of the church."

"Well, we sure are enjoying one another's company today. Estelle, am I detecting an accent?"

"Why, yes. I am originally from Jamaica, West Indies. I left Jamaica when I was fifteen to live with my father and stepmother. Soon after I arrived in New York, my mother died. Unfortunately, I couldn't return home for the funeral. So, I continued to live with my father and his wife, whom I never accepted as a second mother. I had had a mother, and she had just died.

"Father's wife did try to reach out, however; but I didn't want what she was offering. She would buy me things and try, but I wasn't receptive. She did not have children, but I had had a mother.

"My mother was twenty-three when I was born. I am the eldest of five children. My siblings remained in Jamaica and my dad sent money to support our family. It was easy to support a family back in Jamaica, especially for my dad who worked as an engineer for a commercial bus company. In those days, that was something special. My father was pretty smart.

"When I was twenty years old, I was properly introduced to a Jamaican doctor who was fifteen years my senior. We became engaged and were married. My husband was quiet and laid back. Yes, the love of my life, Dr. Vincent Hudspeth, was Jamaican-born and educated in England. Although our marriage wasn't arranged, it was approved by both families.

"The women in my home church were supportive, while the women in his home church in the Bronx were absolutely appalled that he passed over them. What can I say? I joined him in attending the Bronx church because the Bible says 'leave and cleave.' After we were married, I enrolled in nursing school, but that was interrupted by our move to the midwest."

Estelle leaned close to me and added, "They had just begun to give me difficulty when he took the new job."

In just that moment, my suspicions were confirmed and a special bond was established.

She continued. "When I reached the midwest, it took a while before I was accepted by the wives of the other doctors. They were older and born in the United States. So, I joined the Jamaican Club. The club was made up of young doctors and lawyers and their wives who were mostly born in America of Jamaican parents, and did not want to lose touch with Jamaican customs and culture.

"It was sort of like an African American Jack-and-Jill Club [consisting of African American children and their parents who were very successful but had concerns that their acculturation would not afford their children the ability to relate to their culture]. Like the Jack and Jills, many of the members of the Jamaican club were professionals who wanted to embrace Jamaican values and culture. We had dues of $30.00 per month and would have parties to raise money for investments in Jamaica and travel home.

"That was the day! We danced, unlike the church folk here in the United States. Every six months we would have a grand party. We would charge for admission to the party and a fee per plate. The older women would cook traditional dishes like curried goat, rice and peas in coconut milk, roti, patties, fried plantain, ackee and salt fish, fish soup, oxtails, jerk chicken, and bammy."

Enthralled by her reminiscing of food-centered get-togethers, I exclaimed, "Estelle, I love roti, patties, ackee and salt fish, and jerk chicken. Um, um, um. But, what is bammy?"

"You have never had bammy? Well, bammy is a staple in many places in the world. It comes from a poisonous cassava plant that takes eight months of warm weather to grow. We grate the root, then place it in a press overnight. During the night, a white milky substance will drain out of the root. The poisonous milk has to be extracted properly. Once the milk is extracted, you will find a powdery, white, flour-like substance that we use to make fried bread. Of course, we soak the dough in coconut milk before we fry it, and then apply butter before we eat the bread. Ummm, ummm good!"

"Oh my goodness! It sounds good … and fattening, too. Estelle, what happens if you eat the poison? Does it affect your nervous system?"

"Well, perhaps. A person would suffer from asphyxiation at the cellular level."

"Your cells suffocate? That's terrible!"

"All I know is that enough bitter Cassava can kill a cow."

I continued to listen to Estelle's stories about her cherished fellowship and food until the sun was almost set.

"Estelle, I don't mean to interrupt you, but perhaps you would like to select a worship thought. Let me call Robert and the children in."

Jason went to the piano and Robert reached for a few hymnals. We sang a song of thanksgiving and allowed our guest to present the worship thought. She spoke about King David, a man after God's heart.

After worship, Aaron and Jason begged out of going with us to take Estelle home. We agreed. It was not unusual for a Caribbean woman of Estelle's age not to drive. When we arrived at Estelle's apartment, she thanked me for my listening ear, noting that she now felt better than at any time since her now-in-remission cancer had been diagnosed. I assured her that that was what one sister should do for another.

On the way home, we picked up some fruit, snacks, and ice for our customary Sunday family picnic. These picnics had become so much a part of our family routine that we all looked forward to them eagerly.

The next day the picnic was short, but sweet. We rode our bicycles down a colorful tree-covered ten-mile path and had lunch at a table near the lake. After lunch, we returned home. Aaron and Jason had homework. I had laundry and lesson plans to complete. The next morning would come quickly, a time when I would separate from my own children and face my many other children at work.

We were one month into the school year and the students were beginning to settle into their usual modes of behaving. I found this to be true especially on Mondays, when they were filled with energy from their restful weekends. After climbing three flights of stairs, I turned the key in the door that led to the three-office suite I shared with a social worker and a psychologist.

"Good morning, Mrs. Kolinsky. Did you preach yesterday?"

"No, Mrs. Johnson; did you sing yesterday?"

"Of course not, Mrs. Kolinsky. How ridiculous!"

This was our morning ritual. Mrs. Kolinsky, our psychologist, was an elder at her church. But who would think so? She was a meek, little Caucasian woman, in her 50s who could just manage to squeak out a little voice when she spoke.

On the other hand, I, a speech and language pathologist, wasn't shy at all. Ironically, although I teach many to speak publicly; I myself have a public singing phobia. I also teach public speaking at the community college.

Last school year, I was asked to do a solo for a holiday concert. Wanting to conquer my fears, I acquiesced. So without the knowledge of the choir director, I signed up for singing lessons. My solo was near the end of the concert and flawless. I managed to hold it together until the concert was over. Then I hid in the basement and had a panic attack. Can you imagine that? A panic attack! How hilarious!

I entered my office, unloaded my brief case and a rolling case, scurried out the door just past the girls' restroom, and entered the staff restroom. Mrs. Jones, the social worker, was washing her hands and had her large *somebody's in trouble* expression on her face.

"Good morning, Mrs. Johnson. We have a new student and she will need social work and speech intervention as well as related services."

"Is that so, Mrs. Jones? I can't wait to meet her." Just then, Mrs. Jones pointed her nose upward and drew three sniffs of air into her lungs. You would think that that was something she wouldn't want to do while standing in a public restroom, but this woman had extraordinary olfactory senses.

"I smell smoke." And she made a beeline out of the restroom and into the girls' restroom next to ours. I followed.

Upon entering the room, I saw an attractive student waving her hands in a futile effort to dissipate the smog-like haze in the air. She had obviously flushed her cigarette butt down the toilet. Busted on her first day of school.

Mrs. Jones turned to me and said with her wicked smile, "Mrs. Johnson, this is your new student, Eileen."

Eileen wore a stiff French roll and a little too much make-up. She was about 5 feet, 9 inches tall and carried a purse on her one arm which was paralyzed in an upward position as if it were a hook. A sixteen-year old ninth grader, she had missed two years of school as a result of being in a coma for nine months after being brutally beaten and stomped by a group of women [monsters, really].

After coming out of the coma, Eileen had undergone rehabilitation to learn to walk, use the restroom volitionally, feed and dress herself, and speak. Now it was up to me to help her with deduction, judgment and pragmatics, and extinguishing her lack of inhibitions.

I invited Eileen to accompany me to my office. She was intriguing. Traces of the disinhibition brought about by her closed head injury were evident in her spontaneous speaking and gestures. She spoke before thinking, revealed far too much personal information, touched everything on my desk, and asked inappropriate questions. Yet, one could clearly see that she remained a girly girl who always carried a purse and wanted to keep her hair and nails "did."

When asked why she had been beaten into a coma, she admitted that she used to get the men in her neighborhood to give her money for hair, nails, and clothes. The men's girl friends jumped her. The police said that there wasn't anything they could do because she wasn't conscious to identify the assailants. Amazing!

What wasn't amazing was the speed in which she reached a certain comfort level with me. This was also characteristic of someone with her diagnosis. We agreed to meet weekly and began our work for the day. Eileen slowed down after about twenty minutes. She was experiencing predictable neuro-fatigue; so it was time to end the session.

Walking Eileen to class after our first session was necessary, seeing that students with closed-head injuries often have problems with impulsivity and making inappropriate decisions. Dr. Saunders, the principal, approached as we reached her classroom.

I greeted him with a "Good morning, Dr. Saunders."

"Good morning, Mrs. Johnson," he responded. As Eileen scooted into her class, I thought I saw her ingest a significant amount of mucus, but I wasn't sure. Dr. Saunders inquired about the same thing.

My experience suggested that principals were not well versed in the behaviors of some special populations. So I tried to soften his reaction by sharing that Eileen was on the mend from a horrible experience. I shared that she had been beaten into a coma and had suffered trauma to the head which often manifests in unusual behaviors like memory deficits, emotional liability, and difficulties with judgment. Dr. Saunders was taken with compassion as he dropped his head.

Looking up, he said, "Hey! I was in Richmond visiting my sick father for a week this summer and stayed with my sister and her husband. Since my plane did not leave until Sunday morning, I thought just once I would get a chance to relax on a Saturday morning. Instead, my brother-in-law invited me to go to this meeting with him. I thought, "Oh Lord; this is what I get for not staying in a hotel."

"But, you know what? It was a good meeting and there were many similarities between this little town of 100,000 people, and our city of 800,000. Anyway, a group of so-called competent, learned men got together. They were a part of the Richmond Improvement Association and had been studying the violence problem in their town.

"You know, people say that Detroit competes with 'Hotlanta' and Gary, Indiana for the dubious title *murder capital of the world*, but I think it's all propaganda. I found that this little town of Richmond experiences about one homicide every 10 days. Can you believe that? And, the bad thing about it is that it is black-on-black crime. Not to say that black-on-white crime is better. It's just a shame that we haven't learned to honor one another. It is everywhere, I guess; and Frazier High School and its community are no exception."

Just then, Mrs. Strong approached Dr. Saunders to complain about the behavior of a student, and I proceeded down the hall. I administered speech therapy to three more groups of students that morning, but couldn't help thinking of my conversation with Dr. Saunders.

The fifth hour bell rang out, and I barely slipped into the teachers' lounge before the crowd reached the door. Interestingly enough, Dr. Saunders was having lunch in the staff lounge. He wore a camel-colored suit over a crisply starched eggshell white shirt with a rounded collar. His fine brown, rust and green silk necktie stood erectly over his collar pin, then dropped suddenly onto his chest. The medium-sized knot was tightly pulled. There were five round tables in the lounge and the few classroom teachers entering the lounge selected the seats at a table to the left of where Dr. Saunders was seated.

Upon my entering the room, Dr. Saunders called out, "Ah, Mrs. Johnson, join me."

"My pleasure, Dr. Saunders. I have been thinking about our conversation earlier, you know, the one about black-on-black crime."

"Yes, Mrs. Johnson, I was hoping we could continue our conversation."

"Well, Sir. It appears to me that not many people care about how blacks hurt each other. People are aware of black-on-black crime; they just don't seem to care or are unable to do much about it. It seems it serves an overall purpose.

"Women, on the other hand, are very aware, as are men, what women do to other women on a daily basis. Yet, we accept this trash because we are conditioned to believe this is just the way women are – mean and catty. In fact, I believe it gives people pleasure to see us violate each other.

"Eileen's case is extreme I know; but it's everywhere and far more prevalent than black-on-black violence. Frankly, it cuts through race and culture, and many women are guilty. I know I am."

"Johnson, it will never change, so get used to it. Has it never occurred to you that we men need for you women to hurt each other and act foolish. Shoot, if women were to stick together, many a man wouldn't have a place to go at night. We'd all have to clean up our act."

"Well, Sir. It's not just what happens at night. It's what happens in the workplace, in churches, in families, and in our schools."

Before we could continue, the head secretary appeared to tell Dr. Saunders that his supervisor, Ms. Perkins, was here to see him. Off he went. Ms. Perkins commanded respect.

As I continued to eat my lunch, I noticed Ms. Gaines, a counselor, signaling her cronies with her eyes. Ms. Gaines always had staff women around her. They waited to see what she thought and how she would respond before making up their minds about anything. They chose not to sit with Dr. Saunders; however, they were now seemingly throwing eye-darts because Dr. Saunders and I often enjoyed a good conversation.

I wish women like Ms. Gaines would learn to talk about things other than who they don't like. When it comes to conversations limited to he-said, she-said, and other women, I pass. Current events, civic and educational issues, philosophy, politics, sports, and interior design are more my cup of tea.

Conversations I dodge are usually spun off by some controlling woman, mainly a queen bee. I always reject Ms. Gaines' attempts to control me, and I reject queen bees. Furthermore, I refuse to be subservient to any queen's court.

In my usual effort to keep peace, I stood and complimented the women for the fine job they had done with the bake sale and shared that I had to run to meet a group of students.

The afternoon was filled with back-to-back group therapy sessions. Before long, Mrs. Kolinsky was in my doorway predictably bidding me not to sing any solos that evening. My affectionate response was to tell her not to preach like Billy Graham during evening service. We laughed. She left. And so, we ended our day together the same way it had begun – with levity.

After we finished our therapy notes, Mrs. Jones and I accompanied each other to the parking lot before driving our separate ways.

* * *

Belinda Gaston phoned me later that evening, saying, "Beth, I was wondering if you could talk to Cynthia Allen. She has experienced a situation that I thought you could relate to, and she is in despair. Can you call her now?"

"Belinda, I can phone her in about two hours. We are just about to have dinner. Will that be okay?"

"Yes, thank you Beth."

That freed me to enjoy a delightful dinner with Robert and the boys. As we sat around the table, we gave thanks for our food and our blended family.

After dinner, Robert and I cleaned the kitchen together and talked about our days in the office. Robert mentioned that we had an invitation to join his sister and brother-in-law in two weeks for a special Sabbath three hours away in Zurich, a little town with only two traffic lights.

I'd never been to Zurich, but I had heard enough about it to be familiar with the town. It had a vegetarian supermarket the size of our local Farmer Jack, with a natural health remedy and organic foods section. I had also heard other things about this town. They had one McDonald's that had a veggie burger on the menu, one Pizza Hut, one vegan restaurant, and a Chinese restaurant that served vegetarian dishes on the buffet. The town had more churches per capita than we have corner liquor stores or hair salons in Detroit.

Within walking distance of Phillip and Linda, Robert's sister and brother-in-law, were a Lutheran church, a Spanish church, a Filipino church, an African church, an All-Nations church, a Korean church, an African American church, a Caucasian church, and of course the University church. Addison Academy, sister school to my alma mater, Andover Academy, was also in this town. Phillip and Linda were both professors at Addison University.

The invitation was timely because it provided for a much-needed get-away. Thank God, we would also miss a weekend at the *Temple in the Sky*. That last thought reminded me. I had almost forgotten my commitment to call Cynthia Allen.

Chapter 2 – My Sister's Keeper

The bedroom was the most comfortable place to take a private conversation. I climbed the stairs, shut the door, and prayed that the Holy Spirit would give me insight when speaking to Cynthia.

"Hello, Cynthia, this is Beth. Belinda Gaston asked that I phone you. How was your day today?"

"Hello, Sister Beth. I was told that I am going through something similar to what you went through. I don't mean to pry into your personal affairs, but you married Robert Johnson a couple of years ago and I heard that the women at the *Temple in the Sky* were particularly mean to you."

"No, Sister Cynthia, I don't think it's prying. Just about everyone knows some aspects of my situation. Go ahead. No disrespect taken."

"Thank you, Beth. You don't know much of my story because you are new to the *Temple in the Sky*. My parents were active in the church. In fact, my mother was a deaconess and my father a deacon. Something happened, and my father bludgeoned my mother to death with the leg of a dining room table. I was just a young girl of fifteen, and I was so disgraced and confused I still don't know what to do.

"I lost my mother and father all in one appalling day. After that, I could not bear the whispers and stares at the *Temple in the Sky*. Losing my parents was horrifically traumatic; but the social stress that followed was amazingly 'in my face.' When I looked into members' faces, I did not see compassion. I saw judgment. I wasn't as strong as my sister. She remained at the *Temple in the Sky,* but I left in shame.

"Grieved, I went out into the world and did what people do when they turn their backs on God. While doing it, I searched for replacements for my parents and found it in the form of a husband. Consequently, I married a man just like my father and suffered abuse at the hands of my husband.

"We later divorced because the whole reason we had married was wrong. We were not equally yoked. I didn't even understand who I was or what I believed. I was in spiritual and mental disequilibrium. Fortunately, I managed to recognize the abuse.

"I was a prodigal daughter; but on my way back to God, I met a wonderful man and my return was delayed. While in the world, I knew that I couldn't live in the state I was in; so I yearned for a life centered and grounded. Before I returned to God, I told my new boyfriend Billy that I could no longer live the lifestyle we were accustomed to, and I wanted to return to God. He loved me so much that he said he would follow me into whatever lifestyle I wanted. He came with me. When I finally found my way back, there was no fatted calf, no open arms, and no welcome. I was dead to the church.

"After a while, some women got together and invited Billy to lunch. They told him about my parents and included things about me that just weren't true. They suggested he turn his attention to a nicer young lady. [He defended me, however; and we later married.] I felt destroyed all over again. Worse yet was that these were women who called other women sister, yet treated me like I was nothing. Believe me, I was shaken. There was no place I thought I wanted to be other than in the community of the faithful. Yet, my sisters were treating me as if I were God's reject. My soul bled.

"We continued to attend the *Temple in the Sky*; but my husband lost his enthusiasm. His response was that the treachery in our church made treachery in the world look like child's play. I am so bothered by all this, that I am tempted to quit again!"

There was silence on the phone as Cynthia was obviously waiting for a response. In silence, I bowed my head and asked God to speak through me.

"Cynthia," I responded, "What you experienced is very unfortunate and undoubtedly painful. But please understand unrest is not what God intends for you in this matter. Isaiah

26:3 says that God will keep you, Cynthia, in perfect peace when you think on him and trust Him."

After a moment of silence, she replied, "That's difficult to do. I feel so…so, crushed."

"Crushed?"

"Yes, crushed. It's as if I don't matter at all. As if I have no feelings. As if I deserve no happiness."

"Cynthia, what do you want to feel?"

She replied, "I want my heart to stop hurting."

"Cynthia, Psalms 34:18 says that God is near to those who have a broken heart and saves the crushed in spirit. I believe He is closer to you than you think. Keep drawing close to Him and He will respond the same way."

Almost before I was finished, Cynthia protested, "But you don't understand, Beth. I am still devastated."

"Cynthia, have you received less social invitations."

"Yes."

"When you go to church, do you go late and leave early."

"Yes."

"Do you participate in lesson study?"

"No."

"Do you feel a certain coolness when you walk into a room?"

"Yes"

"Was there another woman specifically selected by the group for your husband?"

"Why, yes. This is weird, Beth. How would you know to ask me these questions?"

"I do understand, and I really meant it when I said we have similar stories."

"What happened to you?"

"My youngest child, Jason, was baptized at the *Temple in the Sky*. I had a dinner party and invited seventeen guests. Among those guests was this little dynamo named Candice Appleton. Candice suggested that I should meet Robert Johnson. She began to talk about him.

"Robert happened to be someone my girlfriend Laura Light had dated."

Surprised, Cynthia responded, "Dr. Laura Light?"

"Why, yes," I responded. "Well, of course, I politely dismissed her suggestion by saying, 'No, thank you; I am looking in another direction.'

"But Candice would not leave my house. After the other guests had gone home, she remained. Again she asked me to meet Robert Johnson, and again I declined.

"One day shortly after that exchange, who should phone me but Dr. Light?

"I said to her 'Girl, guess what? Jason was baptized and I invited some of the church members over for dinner and this little woman suggested I meet Robert Johnson. Isn't that the guy you went biking with?'"

"Not only biking, but we played racquet ball, too,"

"As we proceeded in conversation, she discovered that she had two friends who attended the *Temple in the Sky*: Robert Johnson and myself. She tried to convince me to meet him; but I blew her off, so I thought."

Engaged, Cynthia chimed in. "Why yes, any lady knows you don't date someone your friend has dated."

"Exactly," I replied. "However, at this particular time, there was much more to it than that. I was ending a one-year pledge to God to refrain from dating. That time was dedicated to making God my husband. Then one day during the altar prayer, I told God that I wanted a husband who was custom-designed for me, one who would be a priest, provider, and protector to my children. One week later, unbeknownst to me, Dr. Light arranged a blind date. She called to tell me that she had worked out all the details.

"Hearing what she had done flabbergasted me! She said, 'He is going to ask you out for dinner and he is very shy; so you had better accept. I told him to say eight simple words. *Will you go out to dinner with me?*'

"Laura asked if I would be in church the coming weekend, to which I responded, 'No.' I added that my girl friend in Tennessee was expected to be released from the hospital on the weekend. I shared that she did not have a great support system and that I was going there to care for her and her family. And, do you know how she responded?

"She simply said, 'Okay, he will ask when you return.' Laura's words left my memory as soon as I returned the phone to the cradle.

"So! The weekend came. I went to Tennessee for most of the week and then returned home just in time for church. I was sitting in church when this tall stallion of a man walked down the center isle. In my heart, I knew that that was Robert Johnson."

Forgetting all about her own sorrows, Cynthia asked: "Then what happened?"

So, I continued, "And, sure as I was sitting there, I lost sight of him. The next thing I knew, he was sitting next to me wringing his hands. He asked if I knew Laura Light. He said he was a friend of hers. He said that she told him to say something to me.

"He went on and on fumbling with words until he managed to squeeze those eight little words out of his mouth. Once I heard those eight little words, I turned to him and said. 'I was wondering if you could follow directions.'

"Trust me; my response was an ice breaker!"

[By this time, Cynthia was completely into my story. Her laughter was cathartic.]

"He sat next to me for the remainder of the service. And this, my Dear, was the beginning of my woes. Little did I know that all eyes were on me, even to the extent that one of his prospects was hanging over the balcony trying to get a glimpse of this social anomaly.

"Not understanding that our joint presence would be contrary to the Mayflower's informal pecking order, I accepted the date. And, let me tell you. My lack of understanding that we, Robert and I, were a socially anomaly was not the only thing I did not understand. Unaware of social politics at the *Temple in the Sky*, I could not have imagined what I would go through."

Engrossed, Cynthia queried, "What did you go through?"

"Oh, individuals dug into my background. They even doctored my background to fuel their gossip mills.

"And if that weren't bad enough, I had to relive this trauma through Robert. Everyday, he would revile at all the attention he was getting and repeat every ugly thing that was said about me behind my back. Repeating these things massaged his ego; but it kept me reliving the pain.

"Things got so bad I needed antidepressants to handle my crucifixion. I was experiencing dissonance, you know, like when the choir sings a combination of sounds that seem difficult to listen to because they take liberty with conventional musicology. Only this dissonance is an inconsistency between actions and beliefs. In my mind, church people are supposed to embrace and love one another. Some did.

"Unfortunately, others did not. They allowed themselves to be used by the powers; and I, too, was victim to the same powers because I did not keep my eyes on God.

"This created a state of disequilibrium for me because I had thought that church is where one goes to be relieved from the dangers of the world. What I learned was that churches take on the characteristic of the members if their eyes are not fixed on God.

"We are not to look to the left or right. Simply keep our eyes on God and listen for His voice. Yes, Dear, we have very similar stories. It's still painful at times. But I can honestly say that I can laugh at the experience. And just as you laughed with me, one day someone just might laugh with you."

"I certainly hope so," was the first glimmer of hope uttered by Cynthia regarding her dilemma.

I continued with references from God's word. "But enough about me, the Bible gives us wonderful stories to draw upon. I am reminded of the story of Joseph, a bright young man said to have supernatural knowledge. He was given several strong spiritual gifts, and God's anointing was upon him. He wore a beautiful robe, a gift from his father, that symbolized Joseph's future rule over his brothers and that his father was intending to give him not only his inheritance, but the inheritance of special blessings of God as well [Paul Johnson, History of the Jews].

"Joseph's brothers were jealous and threw him into a pit, leaving him to die. Later, one of his older brothers went back for him, but he was already gone. A passing caravan had rescued him only to place him into a life of slavery.

"I can imagine that Joseph, although convinced that God had found favor with him, now wavered in faith and was in utter mental agony. Can you imagine him having flashbacks of his brothers' betrayal? Can you imagine his confusion? He was probably as perplexed as you have been about your situation. But, Cynthia, God takes what men mean for ill will and turns it into gold. Be patient. Truth and providence are always revealed and God is faithful.

"Cynthia, perhaps this is something you may want to commit to prayer. I have a prayer partner with whom I have been praying for years in the early mornings over the phone. You are certainly welcome to pray with me during the early morning hours. Or, better yet, might I recommend Estelle Devereaux as a prayer partner. She loves praying, understands these issues, and is home most of the day.

"We talked a bit more, then ended the call, giving each other our blessings."

Morning came sooner than I imagined. As I dragged out of bed, I paused to thank God for another day. Wednesdays were typically a testing and coordinating day for me. As usual, I took my customary 15 minutes for worship, then brushed my teeth, showered, and pulled my twists back into a pony tail. As scheduled, the phone rang at 5:45 a.m.

"Good morning, Beth. How was your day yesterday?"

It was Elder Frank, my prayer partner. I had met Frank when he was a student in my class at the community college. This was during my single days when I was away from the church. He was single then, too.

At the end of the last class session, he patiently waited for everyone to leave before approaching me about becoming his prayer partner. He explained that a prayer partner was someone you prayed with consistently. Prayer partners share an appointment to speak with God. I thought, why not. Over the last eight years, Frank has certainly had a positive influence on my life.

I told him some concerns about the cares of my life, and then we discussed our political leaders and church leaders, and then Cynthia. Next, he shared a few of his concerns. We then agreed in spirit about what we would present before God.

Although Frank was an elder in a neighboring town, I withheld Cynthia's name, identifying her only as a young lady who has been wounded by the members. Our purposes were to intercede, not snoop; so we would vaguely identify people or say unspoken when it was confidential.

It was Frank's turn to pray. He began, "Father God, creator of heaven and of earth, the only wise God, a God of love, mercy and grace. We come before you this morning to intercede as you have asked us to intercede for one another. We bring this battered and bruised young woman before you. She has been wounded by members who have allowed themselves to be used by the enemy. She is one of your children, Lord.

"Still, with all her hurt, we recognize that you are a God who is able to bring healing and comfort to her through the power of the Holy Spirit. Lord, may she seek your will in her life. May she trust you and have a closer walk with you. We ask that you send someone on your behalf to minister to her so this healing can take place and that she may ask the great question, 'What must I do to be saved?' Lord, we ask for healing upon her entire household. Then, Lord, we ask that you will teach those who have harmed her that you are a loving God, full of compassion, and not willing that one be lost.

"Father God, we humble ourselves before you, knowing that you are a God who sets up and takes down kings and queens. So we trust your leading through our rulers, knowing that you do not make mistakes. You love us so much, and we thank you for your love. We understand that we lack wisdom, so we ask that you will grant our leaders and their counselors wisdom and knowledge. Grant them strength, mercy, empathetic hearts, sympathy, and kindness for those they rule and for those who are affected by their rule. Bless their families and protect them.

"We ask the same thing for our church leaders, oh Lord. Bless our pastors and help them to stay close to you. Bless the work of our elders, deacons, deaconesses, and department heads. Bless the personal ministries of our members and help us to do your will. Beth has asked that you show her her purpose in life; please reveal your perfect will for her life.

"We ask that you protect our individual spouses and help us to be loving mates to them. Bless, protect, and save those in our church family who do not know you in the free pardon of their sins. Help us to be good stewards of the gifts and talents that you have given us. We pray that our lives will be lived for you, that our characters will become more and more like your character, that you will give us pure hearts, and that we may serve you and mankind. Help us to love and to forgive without being asked to do so.

"Help me in today's negotiations Lord. We pray that you would protect the jobs that are at stake. Help the families of the workers to continue to enjoy the blessings that only you have been so kind to give them. Bless Beth's students and defend them against violence and poverty.

"Be with those among us who are sick and suffering. We pray for blessings upon their spiritual health, their emotional health, and their physical health.

"Bless our children. Send your holy angels to protect them and guide them. We pray that they will develop a personal relationship with you and that we will hear your voice and be obedient to you. Help us to be good stewards over our children and all that you have so kindly blessed us with.

"Then, Father God, may we be careful to give you all the praise. We thank you in advance through faith. We thank you for the privilege of approaching your throne. Knowing that only your grace is sufficient to cover our sin and requests, we ask that the words of our mouths and the meditations of our hearts will be acceptable in your sight, oh Lord, our strength, and redeemer. We ask these things in the name of the Father, and the Son, and the Holy Ghost. Amen."

As customary, Frank then added, "Beth, you have a beautiful day." Then he called his next prayer partner. By 7:30, Frank would have been praying for over ninety minutes with 6 different prayer partners. Frank was more than a prayer partner; he had adopted me as a spiritual mentees every since his last class as my student.

After dressing, I kissed my husband. Then off Jason and I went. Jason was accustomed to getting a ride to school with me. Aaron rode the bus with his friends. Before he darted off with Stephen Hillman, he reminded me that he would need my help proofing his history report after school.

Minutes after dropping Jason at school, I arrived at Carter High School, my second school. It was minutes from our home. Working at Carter High, had a cyclic routine: seeing students in groups all day long on Tuesdays and Fridays each week, and testing and coordinating on Wednesdays.

At the top of the morning, I needed information for a report and found myself in the office standing at the long rectangular counter. On the opposite side of the counter was a pool of four secretaries: the principal's personal secretary, a membership secretary, a payroll secretary, and the attendance secretary, the woman holding a conversation with me.

The attendance secretary and I had developed a fondness toward each another. After obtaining the needed information, we lingered just a little longer to exchange tidbits about our life experiences.

To both our disbelief, a young girl ran past the counter into the pool of secretaries in search of a safe haven. Then two twin girls, who blatantly went for bad, also ran past the counter and into the pool of secretaries. Three or four more followed. They knocked the student, Kim, I believe, on the floor and began to kick and stomp her.

I could only think, "My God! That is someone's child; and without further conscious analysis, the attendance secretary rushed toward the pack, and I began peeling the girls off their victim. One of the girls hit the secretary in the face, eliminating her from the fray. I continued to interrupt the cruelty. The other secretaries froze in incredulity.

The ruckus occurred just outside the absent principal's glass door. The victim was still covering her head when we pulled her to her feet. After she stated that she was okay but overwhelmed by the experience, I turned and quickly went back to my office.

Closing the door and reaching for my familiar swivel chair, I began to weep. What would have happened if the girl had run to some remote part of the building? What would have happened if Frank and I had not prayed that God protect students against violence? I was led to reflect on what Paul tells us, "*We wrestle not against flesh and blood, but against principalities, against powers, against the rulers of the darkness of this world, against spiritual wickedness in high places*" [Ephesians 6:12].

With this all-too-recent graphic reminder that the forces motivating the gang of girls were probably demonic, I began to weep and weep some more. I wept for Eileen, my new student with the closed-head injury. I wept for the student in the office.

I wept for Cynthia and Estelle, and I wept for myself. I could no longer deny the cause of this contempt for women. I could no longer place its origin in earthly emotions. I was beginning to understand.

Soon I was able to pull myself together and return to the routine of planning intervention strategies for the new students on my caseload. Before I knew it, it was time for lunch. But who could eat behind such a tumultuous morning? Perhaps, I had not completely pulled myself together after all. Anyway, I decided to check my email and do some online research to assist my son Jason.

Jason had to do a report for history. He had chosen to report on Frederick Douglass. I thought I would print some information for him to use as a reference. When I entered Frederick Douglass into the search engine, I found something from a book called *The Color Line* which impressed me for its depth of insight and its contemporary relevance. Writing in 1881, Douglass refers to the source of hatred and prejudice as an instinctive aversion having its motive and mainspring in some other source apart from race or color. Furthermore, he observes that race issues are just methods of concealment:

> If what is called the instinctive aversion of the white race for the colored, when analyzed, is seen to be the same as that which men feel or have felt toward other objects wholly apart from color; if it should be the same as that sometimes exhibited by the haughty and rich to the humble and poor, the same as the Brahmin feels toward the lower caste, the same as the Norman felt toward the Saxon, the same as that cherished by the Turk against Christians, the same as Christians have felt toward the Jews, the same as that which murders a Christian in Walachia, calls him a 'dog' in Constantinople, ... persecutes a Jew in Berlin, hunts down a socialist in St. Petersburg, drives a Hebrew from a hotel in Saratoga, that scorns the Irishman in London, the same as Catholics once felt for Protestants, the same as that which ***insults, abuses,***

and kills the Chinaman on the Pacific slope – then may we well enough affirm that ***this prejudice really has nothing whatever to do with race ..., and that it has its motive and mainspring in some other source....*** [*The Color Line,* emphasis added]

Douglass' words were stirring deep within as I stared into the air. I could see him deliver this speech with much conviction, wearing pinstriped pants and a crisp white shirt, his black jacket, contrasting with his long thick, kinky, salt-and-pepper hair. The ringing phone interrupted my thoughts. "Hello. Carter High. Beth Johnson speaking. How may I assist you."

"Hi, Beth. I am sorry to phone you at work. This is Estelle Devereaux. I wanted to catch you early in case you were going to prayer meeting tonight."

"How are you, Estelle? What can I do for you?"

"I am having a game night this Saturday. Would you like to attend?"

I remembered that Robert and the boys had plans, so I would be free. Perhaps this is what I needed to take my mind off what happened here today.

"I will be there."

Chapter 3 – Contempt Gone Bad

Before leaving the house on Saturday night, I looked at my Scrabble work book and reviewed my two- and three- letter words. Robert and the boys were on their way to dinner and the Pistons game, and I moved in the direction of Estelle Devereaux's apartment. The guard buzzed me in and invited me to sign the registry. The elevator stopped on the fourth floor. I turned left and walked to the end of the hall.

Estelle answered and showed me where I could place my shoes. Caribbean culture dictated that you remove your shoes when entering someone's home. She introduced me to two young women sitting at a cream marble table above plush cream carpet. The apartment was professionally decorated using cream and red. Large, tall windows surrounded the living room and dining area. The two other guests greeted me cordially, followed by formal introductions from Estelle. "Beth, this is my niece Lisa Smith and my prayer partner Cynthia Allen. We were just about to get started. What would you like to drink? We have ginger beer, ginger ale, cranberry juice, and soda. What's your pleasure?"

"I'll have ginger ale, please."

The Scrabble game started with a bang. Lisa was first. She began with the word 'intern.' "Twelve points, please." Estelle kept score.

Then Cynthia placed the suffix 'alize' after 'intern' making the word 'internalize' which extended her word to the triple word score slot. "One, two, three, four, five, six, seven, eight, nine, nineteen, twenty times three. I'll take 60 points."

Estelle added the score and created the word 'con' by connecting 'co' to the first 'n' in internalize. She added her score.

Stretching my hands across the board I said, "This is something I've been thinking about lately," and added 'tempt' to 'con' making it 'contempt.' The game went on and we enjoyed each others company. After the first game, we took a break for fresh fruit salad, broccoli quiche, and broiled salmon.

Lisa was Estelle's niece and a promising attorney. "Beth," Lisa called. "I noticed you spelled words like contempt and guilty. These are words I deal with. Is there anything on your mind?"

"Wow, you are sharp! How could you tell? I guess it's no secret that I have a passion for the way women ought to treat each other. Well, we heard a sermon about Cain and Abel in church this weekend and I guess I am still affected by it."

"Oh, yes!" Estelle joined in. That was a good sermon. How did you like it Cynthia?"

"I spent most of my time trying to quiet the baby and I missed most of the sermon."

Estelle continued, "The pastor started with a definition of contempt as it relates to the judicial system. The judicial system defines *contempt of court* as any willful disobedience to or disregard of a court order. This disregard usually insults the dignity of the court and is punishable by monetary fines, imprisonment, or both. He said that when the judge perceives someone as challenging or disregarding the court's authority, the judge has the power to declare the defiant person in contempt of court."

Lisa agreed and added, "There are two types of contempt – criminal and civil. Criminal, or direct, contempt happens when the contemnor interferes with the power of the court. Civil, or indirect, contempt happens when a contemnor ignores a court order outside the court. Both criminal and civil contempt are serious."

I agreed and added, "The first couple on earth was Adam and Eve, right? Adam and Eve had children. Of the children they had were Cain and Abel. When Eve became a mother, she hoped that she had given birth to the promised Messiah. Instead, she had birthed the world's first murderer, making murder part of the legacy of earth's first family.

"The idea is that Cain demonstrated contempt, and his contempt went terribly bad. He was a tiller of soil.

"Abel on the other hand, was a keeper of sheep. Cain brought an offering to God that consisted of produce, and Abel brought an offering that consisted of the first-born of his flock. God respected Abel's offering but did not accept Cain's offering. So, Cain was really upset. He felt rejected and depressed. In response, he plotted, then took Abel for a walk and killed him.

"Now the question is: Given the definition of contempt, meaning hatred, derision, scorn, and disdain, was this the first recorded incidence of contempt?"

Estelle and Cynthia agreed that it was, and I listened.

When they were comfortable with their conclusions, I continued by asking, "Or, could the first recorded incidence of contempt be located in Revelation 12, beginning around verse 7?"

Interested, Lisa reached for Estelle's Amplified Bible and began to read.

[7]Then war broke out in heaven; Michael and his angels went forth to battle with the dragon; and the dragon and his angels fought.

[8]But they were defeated, and there was no room found for them in heaven any longer.

[9]And the huge dragon was cast down and out—that age-old serpent, who is called the Devil and Satan, he who is the seducer (deceiver) of all humanity the world over; he was forced out and down to the earth, and his angels were flung out along with him. [Revelation 12: 7-9, Amplified Version]

"I don't know about you, but that seems like contempt to me. I think that when Cain allowed sin to enter his heart, he took on the characteristics of Lucifer. It seems that jealousy and rebellion played a significant part in both Cain and Lucifer's predicaments. Cain was jealous of Abel and angry with God. Lucifer was jealous of Jesus and angry with God. Of course, I believe Lucifer demonstrated the first contempt in heaven and then brought contempt into the earth. Cain's actions made Lucifer and him allies. So, let us return to the definition of contempt. Since God is judge, both Cain and Lucifer could have been held in criminal and civil contempt of court. I say criminal contempt because they both challenged God's authority. I say civil contempt because they both, through betrayal, deliberately sought to hurt God's creatures, namely members of the first family."

Our conversation triggered questions within Cynthia's heart. Unable to contain herself, she drummed the table to the beat of her question, "What makes us harbor hatred?"

"Wow! That's an interesting question. I don't know, but if I am honest with myself, the times I have harbored hatred are the times I wanted to see someone hurt, perhaps as badly or worse than I am hurting. Or, perhaps I simply want someone to disappear. And that's frightening. It's frightening because I realize I can't hate and be close to God at the same time. What do you think, Estelle?"

"It makes me ask, 'With whom are we close when we hate?' Or, worse yet, who is our ally?'"

"Ally?" Lisa begged.

"Yes, ally," replied Estelle. "With whom are we in association? Who is helping us?" Better yet, "Whose common purposes are we working to achieve?" We all sat there. It was too frightening to admit. So we decided to avoid the answer and return to our games.

We returned to the table and Estelle introduced a game called "Rook?" It was interesting and a lot like Bid Whist. I have never been good at Bid Whist, and I wasn't any better at "Rook."

Still, it was good to laugh. After the others left, since Robert and the boys were still out, Estelle and I watched a DVD. After the movie, I phoned Robert to make sure he was home, and then drove uptown toward home.

Robert watched me drive into the garage. Entering the house, I asked, "How was the game, baby?"

"Great!"

"I take it that means we won." Robert wasn't much of a talker. That is, not until we went to bed. Then he seemed to abandon his introversion and become very talkative and cuddly.

I went into the boys' rooms to say good night and hear the highlights of the game. After they tired from talking about the game, I asked Robert to help me with a thought I had about spiritual warfare. "Honey," said I.

"Yes?"

"You fought in the war. And, yet you consider yourself another kind of soldier, a Christian soldier. What would you say are some significant similarities and differences between the war in which you fought and the war we fight daily as Christians?"

"Beth, I often think of what that cruel, but powerful, General Joseph Stalin once said, 'There has been no instance yet in the history of war of the enemy jumping into the abyss of his own accord. To win a war one must lead the enemy to the abyss and push him into it.' When I was a soldier we learned that passage from a publication called the 'Order of the Day.'"

"Interestingly, that was probably true for mere mortals like Stalin and Hitler, but I don't think it was true for Satan. Christian theology presupposes the existence of a heavenly world that also suffered the devastation of warfare. This warfare began with the seedling of personal conflict and mushroomed into a cloud of contempt and hatred.

"Satan committed the worst type of treason against the sovereign God. There was no abyss or hell fire before his treason. However, God will create an abyss for him: hell fire. The instant Satan detected his heart's jealousy of God, he should have submitted himself – that is, surrendered – to the throne of grace, thereby sparing his fellow angels and himself.

"This was not to be, however. Instead, intoxicated with his beauty and position, he allowed pride and appetite for power to lead his fellow angels to the abyss of sin. Then he decisively pushed them into a pit that until then would only be his to occupy.

"Many leaders become absorbed with themselves at the expense of the people they lead. Pride and the desire for power caused Lucifer to become absorbed in all that God had blessed him with. Lucifer defiantly stood face-to-face with the one who created him; as many young people bitterly stand face-to-face with the parents who gave birth to them. Lucifer's limited wisdom, just as the limited wisdom of some adolescents, was far inferior to the wisdom of God. Self-absorbed in his beauty, his spirit was one of insubordinate insolence in his quest for omnipotence."

Robert drew me close to him as he reached for his Bible. "Baby, Satan was like an exceptionally handsome dude who thought he was hot stuff!"

"The Bible describes the appearance of Lucifer, his exotic workmanship of jewels, extraordinary vocal ability, and match-less perfection. Satan had everything your heart could desire. But he wasn't satisfied. He wanted to be God. Now the boomerang is that our heavenly Commander-in-Chief will push the enemy of our souls into the abyss in His great judgment. Let me read from Ezekiel 28:13-19:

13 Thou hast been in Eden the garden of God; every precious stone was thy covering, the sardius, topaz, and the diamond, the beryl, the onyx, and the jasper, the sapphire, the emerald, and the carbuncle, and gold: the workmanship of thy tabrets and of thy pipes was prepared in thee in the day that thou wast created.

14 Thou art the anointed cherub that covereth; and I have set thee so: thou wast upon the holy mountain of God; thou hast walked up and down in the midst of the stones of fire.

15 Thou wast perfect in thy ways from the day that thou wast created, till iniquity was found in thee.

[16] By the multitude of thy merchandise they have filled the midst of thee with violence, and thou hast sinned: therefore I will cast thee as profane out of the mountain of God: and I will destroy thee, O covering cherub, from the midst of the stones of fire.

[17] Thine heart was lifted up because of thy beauty, thou hast corrupted thy wisdom by reason of thy brightness: I will cast thee to the ground, I will lay thee before kings, that they may behold thee.

[18] Thou hast defiled thy sanctuaries by the multitude of thine iniquities, by the iniquity of thy traffick; therefore will I bring forth a fire from the midst of thee, it shall devour thee, and I will bring thee to ashes upon the earth in the sight of all them that behold thee.

[19] All they that know thee among the people shall be astonished at thee: thou shalt be a terror, and never shalt thou be any more.

Robert continued, "You can clearly see the same spirit in the world today. Lucifer was taken with his craftsmanship and position. Don't we do the same thing? We get taken with our assets, power, rank, and position.

"In fact, Beth, I think we can clearly see Lucifer's characteristics present in one of our world's most devastating leaders. Hitler was responsible for killing six million Jews. This was sinister. His hatred was poisonous, not only for the Jews, but also for an estimated 50 million other people who are thought to have lost their lives as a result of his actions."

Robert withdrew his arm from around me to reach for another book from the stack on the floor. Parting the pages he continued, "Here is a statement I read just the other day:

'The evil continued to work until the spirit of disaffection ripened into active revolt. Then there was war in heaven, and Satan, with all who sympathized with him, was cast out. Satan had warred for the mastery in heaven and had lost the battle. God could no longer trust him with honor and supremacy, and these, with the part he had taken in the government of heaven, were taken from him' [White, Selected Messages (1), p.222.4].

"Lucifer was canned! His position in the government of heaven was revoked. Lucifer had been the most powerful angel. It is hard to imagine how much influence he had. One third of God's angels took Lucifer's side against God Almighty. Talk about a no-brainer! It was a confederacy of betrayal."

Robert continued to read.

'Since that time Satan and his army of confederates have been the avowed enemies of God in our world, continually warring against the cause of truth and righteousness. Satan has continued to present to men, as he presented to the angels, his false representations of Christ and of God, and he has won the world to his side.' [White, *Selected Messages* (1), p. 222.3].

"This is why we must die to ourselves daily," Robert commented, "and allow God to lead our lives." After he finished reading, we snuggled in for a good night's sleep.

The next morning, I awakened to an empty place next to me. Robert had gone for his usual hour-long morning prayer-run around our North Park neighborhood. As I reflected on our conversation from the night before, I decided to focus my personal devotion on the same topic: contempt. Thumbing through the book of Matthew, I ran across an interesting story in chapter 14.

1 At that time Herod the governor heard the reports about Jesus,

2 And he said to his attendants, This is John the Baptist; He has been raised from the dead, and that is why the powers of performing miracles are at work in Him.

3 For Herod had arrested John and bound him and put him in prison [to stow him out of the way] on account and for the sake of Herodias, his brother Philip's wife,

4 For John had said to him, It is not lawful or right for you to have her.

5 Although he wished to have him put to death, he was afraid of the people, for they regarded John as a prophet.

6 But when Herod's birthday came, the daughter of Herodias danced in the midst [before the company] and pleased and fascinated Herod,

7And so he promised with an oath to give her whatever she might ask.

8 And she, being put forward and prompted by her mother, said, Give me the head of John the Baptist right here on a platter.

9 And the king was distressed and sorry, but because of his oaths and his guests, he ordered it to be given her;

10 He sent and had John beheaded in the prison.

11And his head was brought in on a platter and given to the little maid, and she brought it to her mother.

12And John's disciples came and took up the body and buried it. Then they went and told Jesus.

I thought, *Wow! Herod's wife really hated John. I guess this hatred was certainly a form of contempt.* If I remember right what Lisa had said, contempt means "hatred, derision, scorn, and disdain." When John had told Herodias that Herod was not her lawful husband and that she was still married to his brother in the sight of God, John in effect publicly pronounced her as an adulteress. At that moment, the powers of darkness that were in control of her passions seized the opportunity to torment Herodias until they used her to accomplish their goals.

In the Garden of Eden, evil had worked through the one whom God meant to be a blessing to accomplish the fall of Adam. Now Herod faced the same fate. John, the mouthpiece of God, became the direct object of Herodias' contempt against God and his law.

Chapter 4 – Needs

Around 5:43 a.m., I finished my personal prayer in time for my telephone appointment. Like clockwork, the phone rang at 5:45.

"Good morning, Beth."

"Good morning, Frank. What is on your heart this morning?"

"I have an unspoken request."

"Anything else?"

"Let us pray that God will order our steps according to his perfect will."

"Anything else?"

"No. How about you, Beth?"

"Yes, I would like to pray for my students, our children, and that God would use us to minister to someone in need."

"Okay let us pray." We prayed and ended our prayer as usual, stating, "We ask that the words of our mouths and the meditations of our hearts will be acceptable in Thy sight, oh Lord, our strength and redeemer. We ask these things in the name of the Father, and the Son, and the Holy Ghost. Amen."

Just then, Aaron knocked at the door. "Mom, we are ready for worship."

We met in the living room as usual. Jason was playing a hymn the family had selected. It was a song my husband was taught in Quang Tre Province, Vietnam, by a United States Army chaplain from Saigon. Robert and the chaplain sat on a grave, watching the sun go down, singing

> Redeemed. How I love to proclaim it,
> Redeemed by the blood of the Lamb.
> Redeemed by His infinite mercy.
> His child and forever I am.

We had all learned to love this song, too. I scooted across the room and sat on the large comfortable sofa.

Robert began by reading the morning passage from Isaiah 61:1.

> The Spirit of the Sovereign LORD is on me,
> because the LORD has anointed me
> to preach good news to the poor.
> He has sent me to bind up the brokenhearted,
> to proclaim freedom for the captives
> and release from darkness for the prisoners ….

Then he told a story about a mean woman and two children. This mean woman, Mrs. Frantz, never came out of the house except at night. She wouldn't speak to her neighbors and wouldn't answer her door. When children would play on her grass, she would knock on the window and shake a stick at them.

One day, upon returning home from school, the children noticed that there was an ambulance at the mean woman's home. They told their parents about the ambulance, and they all went down to the house in concern. The paramedics rolled her outside, and they were followed by a younger woman who appeared very distraught. Once the woman was placed into the ambulance, the young woman jumped into the ambulance, too, and away they went.

The next day, while picking up paper from around the outside of the house, the young woman was approached by a man who offered to cut the grass and remove sales papers while Mrs. Frantz was in the hospital.

The young woman introduced herself as Gail Frantz, his neighbor's daughter. Gail was visiting her mother from out of town and would soon return home. She shared that her father and brother had been killed by a robber fourteen years ago, and her mother has pushed everyone away from her ever since.

Robert explained that the woman really wasn't mean. Rather, she was broken-hearted and blamed God for her misfortune. The children, looking at a woman shaking a stick at them, were simply the recipients of her anger toward God for allowing her husband and son to be killed.

Robert continued by explaining that the Mrs. Frantz of the story was really Mrs. Blumfeld who lived on our very own street. He asked if we would adopt Mrs. Blumfeld and ask that God would free her from her prison of sorrow. We all agreed and lifted her name up in prayer.

After school that day, the children and I went out to our flower garden, picked some Black-eyed Susan flowers, and placed them in a rust-colored vase. Robert and the boys took them to the hospital for Mrs. Blumfeld while I prepared dinner. Black-eyed Susans were one of Estelle Devereaux' favorite flowers, so I asked the boys to remember to take some of them to the next divine service for her. I would have called her to see if she wanted them at that time, but it was around the time of evening for her prayer ministry with Cynthia Allen.

* * *

Taking the time to speak with a co-worker in need, Cynthia stayed at work later than she had anticipated and was late picking the children up from school. Mrs. Hanes, the assistant principal, expressed her displeasure as Cynthia rushed into the building to collect her children.

On the way home, she called the local pizza parlor, ordering two deluxe vegetable pizzas and a Greek salad in fear that she would not be ready for her prayer session with Estelle Devereaux. She was finding the sessions to be uplifting and took seriously their appointment to speak with God.

Arriving home, she immediately placed the pizza on an attractive platter and half the salad on each matching bowl for the children. They said grace and began to eat dinner.

Cynthia's husband was out of town on a business trip. After dinner, she asked the children to spend the next half hour either reading library books or by beginning their homework. She went into her bedroom and shut the door.

Picking up the phone, she dialed Estelle's cell number. "Hello, good evening" answered Estelle, as was her custom.

Cynthia began, somewhat out of breath, "Hello Estelle. Today I spoke with a co-worker who was tortured about a relationship she was having with a married man. She had fallen in love with him. He is the husband of the woman's friend and the woman had not meant for the relationship to become so involved.

"The married couple began having difficulties during a time that the wife was angry with her friend. The husband sought out my co-worker to ask advice, and she sympathized with the husband. This sympathy created a bond between them and one thing led to another.

"Now the wife has reached out to her friend, my co-worker, and apologized to her because she needed to confide in someone in fear of losing her mind. The wife is in despair, and my co-worker realizes she could lose both her lover and her friend.

"I have been so focused on my pain that I failed to realize that there are others around me who are also suffering.

"Let's pray for them by name. What is the wife's name?" asked Estelle.

"Sue."

"What is her husband's name?"

"Preston."

"Are there any children involved?"

"Yes, plus the wife is two months pregnant. But, my question is how do I minister to Wilma?"

"Listen to her. Let her talk. Pray for her and with her. The Holy Spirit will speak to her and convict her. Just be there to reinforce His leading.

"In addition, Cynthia, you might want to reference the story of Sarah and Hagar found in Genesis 21. Sarah, the wife of Abraham, along with her husband, was promised a son by God. Sarah's biological clock was not only ticking; but it was so old that it was borderline antique. Well, ten years passed and no son. Needless to say, she had grown inpatient. In her impatience, she decided to take matters into her own hands by giving her husband one of her young maids, Hagar, so that Abraham and Hagar, could conceive a child.

"Sarah's plan was to raise this child with Abraham. This was a mistake. Worse still, Sarah, who was actually chosen by God to become the mother of the Promised Child, became jealous, insecure, and angry. Hagar, who was chosen by Sarah, became boastful, proud, and haughty. At that time, Sarah's character left much to be desired. Sarah trusted Sarah and not God who is consistent in His promises and institutions. He created marriage and He upholds marriage. Even though Sarah created a mess of the situation by being impatient and distrusting God, God blessed both Hagar's son and Sarah's son.

"Preston should have trusted God and sought sound counsel. This counsel could come from his minister, a professional counselor, or preferably an older man with solid Christian character. Preston's wife should have done the same. And, if she were to confide in someone, it should have been an older woman of solid Christian character."

"Wilma, on the other hand should never have entered into confidence with Preston when she had strife with his wife. She was engaging in dangerous cross-sex counseling with a vulnerable party and was not emotionally or spiritually stable to give counsel."

"Estelle, I should mention that Wilma is pregnant too."

"My Lord! We will keep this situation before the altar. Believe you me; I know how painful this can be, and it is so unfair to the children. Cynthia, are you ready to pray?"

"Yes."

"Let us seek the Lord in prayer."

While Cynthia and Estelle were talking, I was across town staring out the window above the kitchen sink when Robert's long arms reached down and around me with a warm embrace.

"The boys and I are about to leave and I thought we could pray first."

"Sure."

"Heavenly Father, please help Mrs. Blumfeld to recover from her illness. Supply her needs and cause her heart to rejoice in your love, and thank you for leading us to her. Amen."

Robert, Aaron and Jason said good-bye and ten minutes later walked down the long corridor of the 4th floor of the Baymount Hospital into Mrs. Blumfeld's room. She was delighted to have company. Staring at the Black-eyed Susan flowers, tears welled up in her eyes. They were her favorite; and she hadn't had a flower garden since her husband and son were killed. As much as Mrs. Blumfeld appreciated the flowers, she appreciated Robert and the boys even more. She placed the flowers on a table near the center of the room so they might also be enjoyed by her roommate who was out of the room at the time.

Mrs. Blumfeld's son and husband had been owners of a local business and at closing time forgot to lock the doors. They were robbed at gun point by two men under the influence of drugs. Unfortunately, Mr. Blumfeld resisted; and in a scuffle, the gun went off. The gunmen then killed his son in fear of leaving a witness. Cameras filmed the entire incident.

When Robert and the boys reached home, they were welcomed by the aroma of Italian bread and tuna casserole. A large tossed salad with bright red tomatoes, cucumbers, red onions, and avocados sat on the table next to some Black-eyed Susans in a crystal vase. After grace, we began with the salad. Over dinner, Robert discussed their visit to the Baymount hospital to see Mrs. Blumfeld.

I sat staring out the kitchen window at the red and orange leaves on the nearby trees and thought about how Mrs. Blumfeld must feel.

I thought about how Eileen and Kim must feel. My mind flashed back to the time my mother had to pick me up from grade school because girls threatened to fight me. I thought about Cynthia, Estelle, and my own mother.

Just then, Robert's voice was heard, "Honey, what are you thinking about?"

"Baby, there is so much contempt in this world."

"Yes Beth, but what man means for ill, God can use for triumph. Is there anything else on your mind?"

"Well, yes there is, Robert. I want to go back to school to study human behavior."

"You should, Beth. You should."

Chapter 5 – Old Dog, New Tricks

Dr. Kaufman, wonderful former adviser and noted authority in the field of Psychology, had not changed much. Since we last met four years earlier, grey had begun to dominate the hair covering the temples abutting each side of his intense face. In fact, his face appeared just as intense now as it had when I left the program four years earlier.

Not sure if my unscheduled appearance would be an inconvenience, I asked "May I enter?"

"Well if this isn't a pleasant surprise! Beth Johnson, how are you?"

"I am doing just fine, Dr. Kaufman. I am here because I was wondering if I can return to the program."

"I never wanted you to leave the program, Beth. There will be paperwork to complete, but I think it's doable. I am curious as to what brings you back."

I shared my concern about Eileen and Kim. I linked their behavior to black-on-black crime and lamented that no one seems to care. I cared and I wanted to do something about it.

After we discussed the problem for an hour, Dr. Kaufman suggested I register for three credit hours of independent study in Advanced Research Design. He would supervise the study. We also talked about an elective, The Psychology of Women.

The Psychology of Women was meeting in a few hours, giving me time to register on-line and return to Dr. Kaufman's office to draw up a course contract for my independent study.

Typically, a three-credit-hour course would require three major assignments. Because I wanted to focus on qualitative design; Dr. Kaufman suggested I create a paper discussing many types of qualitative research, a way of measuring ideas and events by words; at the same time, I would not totally ignore quantitative research, which measures ideas and events by numbers. Included in the paper would be the pros and cons of the qualitative and the quantitative research methods, the best practice for using each method, and an example of each.

Next, we decided that the best course for what I wanted to investigate would be focus group research. So I should pay particular attention to focus groups in my paper. Then, finally, I suggested I conduct two focus groups to see if women perceived abuse between women. That would count for my second and third assignment. And, to think I wanted to do this all along. It would certainly set up my dissertation study. How wonderful!

This would mean lots of painstaking work, of course. First, I would have to read many books and articles on qualitative methods and write the paper. Second, I would have to advertise for women willing to participate in the focus groups. Third, I would have to find someone qualified and objective to help transcribe the tape recording of the group sessions. The transcribing alone would take several days. Finally, I would have to analyze the results of both groups, then defend them to Dr. Kaufman in an oral defense.

Just thinking of analyzing the results was exciting! [I know, I'm quirky that way. But, I could not wait to tell Robert.]

When I returned home, the garage door was up and tools were on the floor. Robert and the boys were not in the yard or in the house. The yard was free of the leaves that had fallen the day before, and the lawn was immaculate.

Just then, I saw Aaron, waving his hand vigorously, motioning that I should move in his direction. Robert and he were clearing the leaves from and cutting Mrs. Blumfeld's lawn. Jason was clearing the withering flowers and planting Annabelle, Carnegie, and Delft Blue hyacinth bulbs for the next spring. I saw a frail little woman appear on the porch – Mrs. Blumfeld.

In a quivering voice, she thanked me for sending the Black-eyed Susan flowers and for allowing my family to help her. I assured her that she was most welcome! I introduced myself, reached into my purse, pulled out a slip of paper, and wrote our phone number down. I gave the paper to Mrs. Blumfeld and asked that she call if she needed anything, and she disappeared behind the heavy wooden door.

I returned home and put some beautiful pink salmon filets on the outside grill, pulled out the pasta salad prepared the night before, and made some coleslaw from green cabbage, traces of red cabbage, carrots, and crushed pineapple. After a few minutes, I made some orange honey glaze for the salmon and brushed it onto the fish that was on the grill. As I closed the lid, Aaron, Jason, and Robert were heading up the driveway.

"Are you hungry?" I asked.

"Are you kidding?" Robert responded.

"Dinner will be ready in twenty minutes. Will you?"

"We are going to wash up now."

I wanted to hear about the boys' day, so I put off telling them about my new classes. Jason talked about his upcoming science project, and Aaron talked about girls. Robert shared that he had to go to the Loraine Ohio plant in the morning and would turn in a little early that evening. Worship would be my responsibility the next morning.

Now it was my turn. I shared that I had returned to school and was fortunate enough to enroll on the last possible day for this semester and that I was able to design one of my classes.

The boys chuckled and said that I would have to sit at the dining room table with them and do homework every night. No excuses. Robert rubbed my thigh under the table and said how happy he was for me. We went to bed early that night.

The next day, on my way home from school, I stopped by the University library and checked out several books for my research paper. After reaching home, I emailed church secretaries in the surrounding areas asking that they enter this ad in their bulletins:

Women of any Age and Race Wanted
for a focus group research on abuse among women:

DATE: October 21
TIME: 6:00 in the evening.

Ten dollar voucher given along with free cosmetics.
If interested, call Beth Johnson at (313) 555-0923.

I also posted the ad around the University and in the staff lounges where I work. I then phoned my friend, Dr. Erin Warren, to ask her to assist with the transcripts. She had asked a favor of me several years earlier when she was working on her terminal degree.

Her response, "So you are finally going to become a scholar?" We chuckled and she shared some of her school experiences. I reviewed the events leading up to my decision and my actions to prepare for the focus groups. She assured me that she would be there to assist me however she could.

Chapter 6 – The Focus Group

The doorbell rang and in walked Angel, a tall, stunningly beautiful woman with very short, coal black hair, bearing a Fifth-Avenue cut. Angel worked for a Fortune 500 company in the area of Information Technology. Her personality was sparkling, and she was very animated.

Dr. Erin Warren followed, bringing moral support. Erin also handled the digital recording of the session. Next, entered Eunice and Felicia. Eunice was of a modest demeanor. Felicia smiled constantly, but never showed her teeth.

Penny, a private school administrator, approached the door at the same time as Elisa. Elisa was tall, polished, and worked for a major automobile manufacturer in corporate education. Bertha, a charter school teacher, entered next. Gwen, a retired public school teacher, followed, thoroughly engaging every one of these ladies in ice-breaking small talk.

The doorbell rang again, and a second wave of guests arrived. In came Dorothy, a jolly, disabled factory worker. Then Wilma came. She appeared ordinary and blended with the group superbly well. Last to arrive was the most stunning of them all: Melanie was graceful and alluring.

They all sat around the large rectangular table. On the middle of the table were a tape recorder and some pastries, sandwiches, fruit, and bottles of water. Questionnaires asking basic demographic information were turned downward, and a gift box filled with skin care items was placed in front of each chair. I began by explaining the purpose of the surveys and asking the ladies to complete the brief survey on the table in front of them. Later, when I tabulated the questionnaires, I found that this focus group had the following distribution of relevant demographics:

Age Distribution of Respondents

Age Range	Respondents
20 to 29	2
30 to 39	2
40 to 49	2
50 to 59	3
60 and up	1

Income Distribution of Respondents

Income Level	Respondents
Less than $20,000	2
$20,000 to $34,999	3
$35,000 to $49,999	1
$50,000 to $64,000	1
$65,000 to $79,999	1
$80,000 to $99,999	2

Employment Distribution of Respondents

Employment Field	Respondents
Technical	1
Education	3
Service	1
Business	1
Manufacturing	1
Clerical	1
Unemployed	2

While they were completing the surveys, I asked if anyone knew what a focus group was or if anyone had had experience with a focus group. One lady responded, "I work in industry. We use focus groups to get information or opinions on new products. We gather a group of people from our target market and let them try the product. We sometimes sit them around a table like this one and have them discuss the product. The group then discusses their experiences and answers questions. We, the manufacturer, then use the information in order to make decisions."

"Excellent! And, this is exactly what we are going to do today. I invited you here to participate in a focus group. A focus group typically consists of 8 to 12 people and that is exactly what we have here today. Instead of product development, we will focus on thoughts and experiences, or–shall I say–a topic that I am very interested in. I ask that you not talk at the same time because we are recording the session. We are going to discuss three questions. I am going to have the session transcribed by Erin Warren [say hello, Dr. Warren], who is a speech pathologist and linguist. Talk as much as you like. That's a good thing. The more information we get the better.

"Your actual name will not be associated with what you say. So please do not write your name on the survey. Feel free to be honest and share your experiences as they relate to three questions that will be asked here today."

"Are there any questions?"

"No."

"Not from me."

"Un, Un."

"Great, then! May I collect your personal data and we can begin?"

* * *

"Again, my name is Beth Johnson. When I say I am studying Woman-on-Woman Abuse, many people have all sorts of thoughts. They usually respond, 'Woman-on-Woman Abuse? What is that?' Granted, there are several types of abuse, physical, economic, sexual, verbal or psychological; so I want to give a definition of abuse. *Abuse is using power or control to mistreat another.* With that definition we are ready for question one."

Beth: "Give me your thoughts on Question One: What is Woman-on-Woman Abuse?"

Angel: "I never really heard of Woman-on-Woman Abuse. Hum. I guess just what you said: Women abusing women or not being supportive of each other."

Felicia: "It sounds like two or more women hurting each other. I know that men abuse women; but women abusing women. That's different."

Eunice: "I think women have unrealistic expectations of each other and often operate under double standards."

Beth: "Double standards?" I probed.

Eunice: "Yes, double standards. Like last week. A soft spoken woman gave a sermon. During her sermon, she cried and stated that she had a past of which she was not proud. The audience was moved to compassion. After the service, I had lunch with a few of the women who had just accepted the speaker into their group even while they were scorning another woman who had a similar past.

"Now, here is what I mean when I say 'double standard.' Both women supposedly repented of their 'sins' and live lives free of whatever they were supposed to have done. The woman being scorned worked very hard in God's service. The only difference is that she didn't seemingly care what the group thought. She did not seek their approval.

"I believe that only God knows all of our hearts. Only God heard their cries or confessions. But we judge who is repentant and who is not. That alone is like making ourselves equal to God. To me, you cannot decide who God forgives and who He does not. Who are we that God needs our counsel?

"Yet, we issue judgments daily in our own hearts; and we issue them as part of groups, too. Sometimes we buy into judgments that are issued by the stronger woman in popular groups. If I am honest with myself, I would not have come up with that kind of conclusion on my own.

"I felt awkward with the response of these women. More importantly, I regret not saying something or reaching out to the woman scorned. But, like much of my life; I stayed in a place where it was safe and acceptable."

Penny: "To me, Woman-on-Woman Abuse is not being supportive; it is trying to tear another woman down."

Beth: "Clarify what you mean by 'tearing another woman down?'"

Angel: "Yes! Tear her down, displace her, and block her from something that would be a good thing for her. Or sometimes we will find a woman who is troubled and instead of pointing her toward positive changes [like asking 'Have you considered counseling,' or 'This book was really good for me,' or 'My pastor does a really good job mediating'], we make things worse by affirming her bad feelings and adding little digs like: *'Girl, you know that all men are dogs.'* That, to me, is abusive behavior. It does not help any situation. It hurts."

Bertha: "I definitely agree. This kind of thing happens to me all the time. As women, we become accustomed to it and don't even recognize it as abuse. These comments are cruel. But most of the time, they are not even comments really; they are unspoken arrows."

Beth: "Unspoken arrows?" This seemed to be an important point to probe further.

Bertha: "You can feel tension and alienation when you walk into a room. It's a woman thing. I think most women are aware of this at some level. I believe this is why I try to blend-in wherever I go. I try not to overdress or underdress. I try to fit somewhere in the middle. If you offend the leaders, you will never recover. This goes for being smart, too. Do not let on that you are smart unless you offer your intelligence to make the leader look good. Heck, don't let on that you have any special skills unless you are willing to let the leader take credit for it.

"I also think status plays a big part in this. Honey, if there is an imbalance in status, watch out! Or, if one is more secure than the others, watch out! It doesn't take words. It's just out there."

Gwen: "I am not convinced that this is abuse. There are people we like to be around and people we don't like to be around. So what! I like to be around people who have experienced the same thing as me."

Dorothy: "I think it begins even before we enter adulthood. Especially in middle schools where girls get together and they move that one girl out of the group because she's not dressed the same way they are dressed, or because she is prettier or even less attractive. Or, her family is not on the same status level as their family. She is alienated.

"I really believe this behavior starts in grammar school. Then it continues on into high school and spills over into our adult lives. Even in our communities we find ourselves either on the inside or outside of in-crowds. Now circles and groups naturally form; this is human nature. It is when the groups become closed and exclusionary that problems exist. Unfortunately, so many groups are somewhat exclusionary. Exclusion when you are on the inside of a group, feels totally different from exclusion when you are on the outside of a group."

Bertha: "Yeah. Baby! In this town, if you are in a sorority or club; you are in. Or, if you go one of those large popular churches, your chances of getting a promotion are greater. And let's not rule out the benefits of having your child go to a premier school."

Gwen: "I am offended by people who say that my children are treated special because they attend a premier school. All the children in this district had the same opportunity to take the entrance test for the premier schools. I will not apologize because I have always worked with my children to teach them. What I have come to learn is that my children go to school with other children who have parents with values similar to the values of my family."

Angela: "As a single parent, I decided to send my children to private school. My family's response was 'Why would you waste money doing that?'

"Okay, I make a decent living at Generous Motors. It's not lavish or anything. But my sisters have not done as well as I. They have grown accustomed to my financial help and think that I should continue to help them at the expense of my dreams for my children.

"You would think your family would understand that education is important. Yet, I am criticized for sending my kids to private school. I have to think about the future of my kids. I work hard for my children and I shouldn't be made to feel ashamed because of it. To me this is abuse."

Beth: "Is that abusive or not being supportive."

Penny: "A little of both. I think that much of the time; we don't really know when we are being abusive. We don't really understand why we may say the things we say or do the things we do. These issues are one and the same for me; regardless of whether we say support or abuse. Why would you suggest not offering children something better?"

Gwen: "It just sounds to me like you are economically stronger than the other women in your family."

Bertha: "It seems like this is their problem, not yours. Send your children where you choose. Strength, whether economic or otherwise, is a problem for many women."

Beth: "Are you saying that abuse is trying to keep someone from assuming their own strength?"

Bertha: "Strength or power, I don't see a difference. Unfortunately, there are women who have learned that they are powerful and use it to suppress and control others. Once you understand that you were given powerful gifts to fulfill purposeful living, you can understand that other women have powerful gifts, too. Perhaps, when women understand this, they will also learn to rejoice in each other's gifts and purposes."

"What I find particularly sad is that your gifts come from God. So to be jealous of another woman's gifts is really to be dissatisfied with God."

Beth: "Wow! Dissatisfied with God."

Bertha: "Oh yeah, Baby, I believe God shaped and gifted me according to His purposes for my life, then formed me in my mother's womb. We are all marvelously made! God knows us inside and out. He knows every bone in my body. He knit me together bit by bit. He sculpted my nothing into something. He watched me grow from conception to birth and intimately knew all the stages of my life. So, if for some odd reason you don't like me, my purposes or my gifts, your problem is really with my maker. And to prove it, you can look in Psalms 139."

Elisa: "So we make judgments in areas that we really should not, and we play God when we devise our catty schemes."

Eunice: "I find the behavior of mothers who want to control their children, especially their girls, questionable. They make comments like 'Do it or…,' which usually means you are not considered a good girl. I find that parents, mothers especially, often make choices for their daughters that really hurt how they view themselves. Choices like who you are supposed to spend your life loving."

Dorothy: "In defense of mothers, they can sometimes see things we can't."

Elisa: "Yes, I think mother-daughter conflicts are very common and that mothers are not always correct; but I like to think of them as mostly correct. There are exceptions. For instance, to this day my mother and I fight all the time. Consequently, I was not raised by my mother, but my grandmother. I did not learn how to be a mother to my daughter until later in our lives. When she was young, I was busy trying not to get my butt kicked by my husband. Then one day, he beat me so badly, I ended up in a hospital emergency room. At that point, I had had enough! So I left with just the night gown on my back.

"After leaving my husband, I was concerned about my survival and the survival of my children. Trust me, their stomachs didn't stop feeling hunger pangs because I left my husband. I couldn't find work because I was not skilled. So, I had to get on welfare and enroll in school. I was consumed with getting our lives together so that we could simply survive. I missed all the little things I should have been doing to lay the foundation for my daughter's emotional well-being. Thank God for my mother. Although my mother wasn't there for me; she, too, realized her failures and was there for my daughter. And so, the cycle continued. My grandmother took care of me emotionally, and my daughter's grandmother took care of her emotionally."

Bertha: "Honey, I understand. My first husband was a minister, and he beat me, too. As a minister's wife, there are not many people you can turn to. If I were to tell a woman in my congregation, they would not believe me. Eventually, I would be hailed a troubled woman who made up lies about 'the pastor.' The worst part is that the women in the church would have set out to defend him. Thank God for my mother and sisters. They helped me to understand that I did not have to live under my husband's rule when my husband himself was not living under God's rule. They were there for me and my son."

Elisa: "I didn't have sisters; so I created a surrogate family with sisters who were either where I wanted to go or also struggling to make a better life for themselves. Sometimes I can't help think that I sold my daughter out for success. Well, I found success. And, after I became a corporate educator I was up and out by six in the morning and didn't return home until seven-thirty in the evening.

"I sacrificed my relationship with my daughter for success. At a moment's notice, I would pack a bag and fly to some location because the company needed me. I spent tremendous amounts of time in the office. It was inescapable."

Beth: "Help us to understand this inescapable theme."

Elisa: "Well, okay. I know that I am not a part of the Old Boys network. I get this. But, there are women in our office who would sell their souls and yours too for acceptance or acknowledgment from the Old Boys.

"I knew the environment was highly competitive and I stayed there and competed. The betrayal is unbelievable! But why is it that I could recognize betrayal when I was victim to it and not recognize betrayal when I was the perpetrator? I believe I betrayed my daughter's well-being for my success."

Melanie: "I find women hard to deal with – period. They treat me terribly in my church. I feel excluded. My children feel excluded. That is so unfair. My three girls are brilliant, loving and kind. It seems as though no one looks out for me except my daughter's teacher."

Wilma: "I think abusing women can include keeping secrets from friends; particularly when you know that those secrets will destroy them."

Gwen: "Yeah. So, wouldn't keeping such secrets from a friend be considered an act of love."

Beth: "I'm not sure what Wilma and Gwen are saying."

Wilma: "What if you've done something terrible to a friend and if your friend would find out it would destroy her. So, you keep it a secret, right."

Gwen: "Well sure, but it sounds like you really want to tell the secret."

Wilma: "I guess so. But, then I don't."

Gwen: "What would you benefit by telling the secret."

Wilma: "She would know. My conscience would be clear on the one hand, and yet it would cause both of us pain on the other."

Bertha: "I still think there is more to women abusing each other than meets the eye. When we first arrived, we were chatting and mingling with each other. Being friendly, right? I don't mean any harm, but, look at how we looked at Melanie when she came into the room.

"Melanie you are extremely beautiful and we all just stared at you. No one smiled or greeted you warmly."

Melanie: "I am used to that. Okay I am not trying to be funny; but women and men stare at me. Many women decide that they just don't like me right away. Men see me as a sexual challenge. But all in all, my heart aches because all I want to do is be accepted and loved for who I am like everyone else. I don't have a degree, but I make ends meet with my legitimate hustle, hair. Hair ladies, you know the kind that I braid in zillions of little strands."

"Okay, I am on public assistance, but I don't think or act like I am in poverty. I study magazines and listen to people. I get along because I am self-educated. Yet, it feels like I don't belong in either world. I don't belong in the world of poverty, and I don't belong in the world where all the polished people live. Furthermore, it seems as though everyone abuses me. My ex-boyfriend knocked me around. My mother tells me I am not going to be anything. Women shut me out. And men try and get in my panties."

Bertha: "I think we were too busy comparing ourselves to you."

Beth: "Comparing. What does that feel like?"

Bertha: "Well it just seemed like Melanie had it all. That God gave her everything. My skin is smooth and pretty much blemish free. But her skin is flawless. I struggle to keep my hair presentable. But it seems like not one strand on her head is out of place. Her clothes are impeccably crisp and fashionable. She has a presence about her and she seems very confident; but not snobbish."

Beth: "So is this about Melanie or you?"

Bertha: "I guess it was really about me or what I think I lack."

Beth: "Melanie, you stated everyone abuses you. Who abused you first?"

Melanie: "My mother did."

Beth: "Would you care to share?"

Melanie: "Well, sure. Earlier I heard Elisa talk about not giving her daughter enough time. Well, my mother was on welfare also, and she did not go to school or have a legitimate hustle like I do. She made ends meet by having one boyfriend after the other. They would help her with back to school clothes, money for little odds and ends, and they would sometimes help with the rent.

"But when they would begin to look at me in the nasty way, she would end the relationship. After each of her relationships was over, she would treat me badly. I grew up thinking that her break-ups were my fault. She didn't encourage me to do anything positive with my life. My mother was a stay-at-home mother. That did not mean she used her time to care for her kids. We were not cared for educationally or emotionally."

(At that time, I explained that the time was up for question number one and announced question number two.)

Beth: "Question 2. Have you ever been abused by another woman."

Melanie: "My mother was never really into us like most mothers. She never attended parent-teacher conferences or spent time talking to us. She was involved with her boyfriends. They went to bars and had card parties until the wee hours of the morning. Sometimes it was hard to go to sleep. When I woke up in the morning, we had to be quiet because Momma did not want us to wake her boyfriend when we were getting ready for school. Once I told my mother that one of her boyfriends tried to fondle me and she slapped my face and called me a liar."

Elisa: "I can only imagine how that must have felt coming from your mother. I felt abuse when I found out that my best friend had been going with my boyfriend for over a year before he broke things off with me. I was really destroyed when they married three months later. Since that time, I have been cold, detached and distrusting of women.

"I know the devastation it caused me to experience a friend's betrayal. Later, corporate America became my man; and I put my faith and trust in something not of flesh and blood. But, Melanie, almost anything can become a source of hurt. That includes best friends, mothers and the individuals, namely women, in the corporate structure."

Dorothy: "I remember wanting to become a decorator when I was a junior in high school. My mother listened to my counselor who told her that black girls did not make it in decorating. Now this woman may or may not have understood what she was doing. However, her words cut deep and the wound is still there over thirty years later. Today, I settle for decorating flowers for weddings and creating custom center-pieces."

Gwen: "I have always been petite and I have always loved dancing. When I was thinking about a dance career, the same thing happened to me. My counselor told my mother that little black girls did not become ballerinas. To this day, I have season tickets for the ballet and long for what may have been during every performance."

Penny: "I still have a problem with this whole concept of women abusing women. There are weak women and there are strong women. Sometimes the weaker women look to stronger women for leadership. As far as Dorothy and Gwen are concerned, maybe their counselors were just operating under their own value systems."

Dorothy: "I feel as though I was the weaker one and my counselor was the stronger."

Elisa: "The counselors were wrong. The very idea of counseling means you are open to possibilities. But, I question: where were your mothers when these things were being said to you?"

Beth: "Is this abuse?"

Gwen: "It feels like it could have been an abuse of power. I was denied support. My dreams were shattered. I could have been successful. People shouldn't be so negligent in handling the lives and dreams of others. Perhaps she was operating in ignorance, but so were many slave owners. This woman was in a position of authority and influence. She used her influence with reckless abandon."

Penny: "People can give advice, but no one has to take their advice. Your mothers should have countered their influence with influence of her own."

Bertha: "Do weaker women look to stronger women for leadership, or do stronger women impose their wills on weaker women? As a former wife of a pastor, I have seen strong women in the church make all the decisions for weaker women. They, or should I say *we*, become dictators in the name of the

Lord. And the Lord is not in that foolishness. God gives us choices and minds to listen to His will. I have a friend who refused to bow down to the strongest women in her church. As a result, her programs are sabotaged and anyone who is found helping her is ostracized from the main group."

Felicia: "My daughters abuse me all the time. They put me out of their lives, and then they expect the impossible from me when they get into trouble. This simply is not fair. They promise never to place themselves or me in a particular situation and they betray that promise continuously."

Penny: "Your helping your daughters is a choice. You can choose to say I will not adjust to or join you in your foolishness. That was not abuse. It was a choice to be victimized. We all have a responsibility to teach others how to treat us. We can't teach someone to take advantage of us and then claim abuse."

Elisa: "Penny, you don't know what it was because you haven't all the facts. We are listening to each other's feelings."

Eunice: "My worst experience with being abused was when I was young and naive. I was friend to a woman named Monica. Monica and her husband divorced. Later he showed interest in me. I went to Monica and told her that I was attracted to him and that he had asked me out. She said, "Help yourself; I don't want him.""

"Time passed and I began to see Monica's ex-husband. Lo and behold, the wrath of women came down on me. And to make matters worse, she led the charge (*laughs from the women*).

"I was stupid to think she would tell me the truth and even stupider to involve myself with some one else's leftovers. I was ostracized, pushed out of my church office, humiliated and gossiped about. Although ten years have passed, the situation is still very alive in my mind. I don't know if I could have abused Monica or if she could have abused me."

Felicia: "You broke the rules. You never openly go with another woman's man."

Beth: "Openly?"

Felicia: "That's all I have to say."

Angel: "Well, I know that my family gossips about me. They say that I am trying to *be all that*. It really works against my self-esteem when my sisters give me hurtful messages from other members of my family. It seems as though the more I resist their manipulations the worse they get."

Bertha: "We cannot forget the classic wrongdoings women do like gossip, backbiting, and spreading rumors. I have seen lives purposefully destroyed with rumors. Rumors are nasty!"

Beth: "What makes rumors, backbiting, and gossip so nasty?"

Bertha: "Well, once they are out there – I mean spoken – you can never call them back. Truthfully, women put them out there all the time and when we find out they aren't true; we just think; oh well. That is so wrong. Ideally, we should not put them out there. But, if we do, we should try to engage in some damage control. Damage control is very difficult and it shows our character flaws because it says 1) I rushed to judgment, and 2) I am reckless."

Beth: (I then explained that the time was up for question number two, and announced question number three. Question three caused most of the women to gasp for air as it was most unexpected.)

Beth: "Question 3: "Have you ever abused another woman?"

(After a pregnant pause, Angel's jaw lowered as she exhaled.)

Angel: "Wow! I guess I have to confess. I have abused someone. I just wasn't expecting that question.

"I can be so nasty at times. I am not one you want to make angry. I have retaliated on my ex-husband's girlfriend somewhat terribly, knowing full well that she could not have had sexual affairs with my husband on her own doing alone.

"Once I found a copy of her utility bill and it was in my husband's name. So I phoned the utility company on a Thursday evening before a holiday and said that I moved and to please shut off the utilities. I played the loving wife and stuck so close to him that weekend that he wasn't able to go to her rescue. I confronted him the following Monday morning and dared him to rescue her."

Elisa: "I have been with men, told them to forget other women, and called the other women out of their names. Basically, I did the same thing to other women that I perceived my best friend did to me.

"I had married lovers. I spent years telling myself that I was not going to be the one who got hurt. I had one married lover for years and am sure I caused his wife plenty of tears over those years. Overall, I was still angry about getting jilted myself."

Dorothy: "When I was young and stupid I was friends with this couple, right. Well, the husband was my lover, and I was friends with the wife also. I was bold enough to go to the woman's house for dinner and have my shoes off under the table running my foot up his pant leg while I nibbled on the wife's home-cooked food. To date, I still have to confess that one in my prayers. How could I eat the woman's food and seduce her husband right under in her nose?"

Felicia: "How could you abuse another woman if she does not know about the affair?"

Gwen: "Oh, *you* know. Whether you admit it to yourself is another issue. I have been married for forty years and I always knew when my husband strayed. He became disinterested in me. He was always tired.

"On the other hand, I reacted to it by becoming more helpless and ill. I was saying look at me, I need you more. I was saying I can't handle this and used sickness to show my pain.

"But you always know. Admitting it is another issue. I received expensive gifts at the end of his affairs and we would fall madly in love again. That is, until the next affair."

Felicia: "So what happened?"

Gwen: "He got too old to do what he did best. Then, I finally got what was left – him. I cannot begin to tell you how many deaths my soul died."

Elisa: "You know, I believe I sent messages to my daughter that she was not as smart as her big brother. Regrettably, I brag on my son an awful lot. I did the same thing my mother did. When I was growing up, my brother was *Mister Wonderful*. I just can't believe I did the same foolish thing."

Bertha: "I think that I have abused other women by gossip. Once those words are out, they can never be taken back. Once or twice, I know I started a rumor on purpose. Shamefully, I now realize that it is a form of murder."

Beth: "Murder?"

Bertha: "Yes. Gossip murders opportunity, character, trust and most importantly hope. Every time we gossip, we break the commandment that says: 'Thou shall not kill.' Most of us murder and abuse. We justify what we do and judge others who are guilty of the same things we are guilty of. We are pious."

Beth: "Pious?"

Bertha: "Yes, pious. We judge murderers and physical abusers harshly. But they did not wake up one day and become murderers or physical abusers. It was a process. And, might I add, we are a part of this process in thought and in deed.

"Christians walk around thinking we are not like murderers and abusers. But in Romans 7:18-19, Paul says that the good he wants to do he does not do. He basically says he was not capable of doing good. So, why do we walk around like we have it all together? *Please*!"

Elisa: "The most hurtful thing is to have your man cheat on you. It seems as though all the various types of abuses are involved in those destructive affairs. As women, we cannot separate our self-worth and emotions from sex.

"Men separate sex from love, but women don't. Although women understand this, women still continue to have affairs with men without being concerned with what it does to other women and their families.

"Men on the other hand, don't seem to understand or care about the effect affairs have on women and children because all too often it is about their egos. I wish women would learn to be honorable in their dealings with other women, and I wish they would learn to require honor from men.

"But of course, I can say all this after I've done my dirt. Come to think of it, when I was in school their was a small group of ladies that would get together and talk about the married men we were seeing as if it were a legitimate means of financial aid. The men helped us pay tuition and purchase our books. I never cared or considered their wives."

Beth: "Much of this seems to focus around the relationship between men and women instead of women and women."

Dorothy: "Because most of the time there is a man somewhere behind why women don't get along. Some men's egos are stroked by women fighting over them. It makes them feel good. Even when this is not the case, women still secretly resent other women for the men in their lives."

Felicia: "Okay, you are right, men are not always involved. We don't like each other based on our baggage which includes insecurity, lack of help, our financial inferiority, and whatever. Face it; not having a man only makes already existing problems seem bigger."

Gwen: "How can you separate the two?"

Eunice: "You have to be really honest with yourself."

Elisa: "I believe that women are awful to each other independently of any other factor. But when you factor a man into the equation, it's a deadly combination of poison. And, this poison paralyzes the soul."

Gwen: "But, is this still abuse?"

Penny: "When we first began, I was skeptical. However, I keep asking myself that same question and I keep thinking about my cousin, Joyce. Joyce has really run her body down. She abuses alcohol and drugs and although 38 years old, she looks much older. She doesn't eat well and she doesn't bathe. She smokes cigarettes. Her lips, skin and nails are real dark. So, does she abuse herself? I think so. Does she honor or respect herself? Now, I consider that self-abuse."

"So, if someone doesn't honor or respect you and it causes harm; I guess that, too, can be considered misuse or maybe even abuse."

Angel: "I accept that I have been abused by other women. But, I am horrified to realize that I abuse also."

Gwen: "Yeah! We abuse our daughters, our sisters and other women. Why do we do this? And, what can we do about it?"

Beth: (Smiling at Gwen's question, I called time on the question and the tape recorder was turned off. To my surprise, conversation in the room burst forth with honesty as secrets were revealed.)

* * *

Dr. Warren inhaled, placed her hand over the right side of her face. Pushing the air from her diaphragm, she exclaimed: "Beth, you got really good information; but the really critical information came after the recorder was turned off. WOW!"

"I know, Dr. Warren. I had to write so fast and try not to be so obvious as to stop the flow of information."

Obviously impressed with the session, Dr. Warren suggested, "I will start transcribing the session so that you can analyze it. By the way, I will do the first transcript and you can do the next one. Try to get the ladies to open up more and probe more."

"Great! Thank you, Dr. Warren," I said. "I have a group next Tuesday. You know, this type of group reminds me of doing a language sample, only I am analyzing it for themes instead of language structures. I guess you *can* teach an old dog new tricks. Perhaps over time, I can get enough information to have a panel of expert judges decide what is and is not abuse between women."

"That's exactly what I was thinking; but, you can also scale and test the results," Dr. Warren added.

Chapter 7 – The Covering

Morning came too soon. Like clockwork, the phone rang at 5:45. I was always glad to hear Frank's customary greeting, "Good morning, Beth."

"Good morning, Frank. What is on your mind this morning?"

"I would like to pray that we be led by the power of the Holy Spirit. And pray that all things work together for good for us and our house. Pray that we love the Lord more and more. Ask that God consider the needs of our family members. Also, pray that we be good stewards of all that God has given us. And, let us pray for the sick among us. What about you Beth?"

"That about covers it, except also pray that God uses me as an instrument to help women."

"Okay, are you ready?"

"Hold on while I get on my knees…. I'm ready."

I prayed first, "Father God, from whom all blessings flow, we humbly approach your throne this morning praising you for being Jehovah-jireh, the Lord who will provide for us, His children. We thank you Jehovah-nissi for placing us under your banner.

"Jehovah-Elohim, almighty God, we thank you for accepting us into your royal family. We thank you for drawing us near to you. We praise you for being all-powerful, all-knowing, and always present. You are a God whose ears are able to hear and whose heart is willing to rescue.

"We come before you today, not only with praise and thanksgiving; but, we also come before you in obedience to your command that we ask, seek and knock at heaven's doors.

"We pray, Father, that your Spirit will lead us. We claim your promise that 'all things work together for good for them that love you and are called according to your purpose.' Please know, Lord, that we love you. But our love can in no wise compare to your love. Help us to love you more and more as we place ourselves in your perfect purpose. Please work for our good.

"We ask that you consider the needs of our families. Please keep them in your ark of safety. Help us to be good stewards of all that you have given us. We pray, Lord, that you, Jehovah-rapha, will heal the sick among us, even those who don't know that they are sick.

"Please help regulate Brother Pete's blood sugar. Please help Mrs. Walter in her struggle with cancer. Lord, in Jesus name, we ask that you take away the radical cells that are attacking her body.

"Help my friend Estelle, who continues to look poorly, Lord. Be with Victor, who is out of prison. Lord, help him to stay away from crime and help him to cling to his new church family.

"We ask for physical, spiritual and emotional healing for my neighbor, Mrs. Blumfeld.

"Please help me to be an instrument to help women to understand how the enemy uses us to kill, steal, and destroy.

"We thank you for answering this prayer; and we ask that the words of our mouths and the meditations of our hearts will be acceptable in your sight, O Lord, our strength and Redeemer. We ask this prayer in the name of the Father and the Son and the Holy Ghost. Amen."

"Amen," echoed Frank. "Thank you for praying. I will call again tomorrow."

* * *

It was fourth Wednesday of the month and time for professional development day for speech pathologists. Instead of going into the schools, I reported to the Serbian Hall for an all-day meeting. A presenter from the American Association for Speech and Language Pathology discussed current trends in our profession in the morning. Two other resource persons presented new test materials in the afternoon.

After the meeting, I drove to the University. I parked far away from my building so I could enjoy a brisk walk after sitting all day.

* * *

I climbed the stairs to Dr. Kaufman's office. Even though his door was ajar, I decided to knock and ask, "May I enter?"

"Come in Beth," was his welcoming reply.

Dr. Kaufman's spacious office was appropriately decorated with rich, masculine browns and thousands of neatly arranged volumes of wisdom in psychology and other fields, I wondered if Dr. Kaufman employed a librarian to keep the collection so neat and well organized.

As I glanced around the room, I noticed that he had a visitor, my other professor, Dr. Lipscomb, an internationally recognized expert in Psychology and Leadership. I had taken a class from her during my first tour at the University. "I am sorry; I did not mean to interrupt you and Dr. Lipscomb. I will come back later."

"No, Beth, this is a good time."

"Thank you. Dr. Kaufman, I was wondering if you were able to look at my transcripts."

"Not only did I have time to look at them. Dr. Lipscomb tells me that you have some interesting finds in your focus group. She tells me that you want to continue to work with some of your participants in a group."

I was grateful for Dr. Kaufman's feedback. He continued, "We think it is a good idea. You can do this either as your project in The Psychology of Women, an Advanced Research II independent study, or if your proposal is ready, you can do this using one dissertation credit. It's your choice.

"You would, of course, be bound to ethical standards. We would like a brief write-up on each woman, including diagnostic factors. I would also like for you to get permission from the Human Subjects Committee to conduct this group if you plan to use any data from it at a later date.

"Now, let's see… Ummm. You would have to choose a co-leader so that processing can be as objective as possible. Why don't you meet with Dr. Lipscomb later to work out the details?"

"Oh, yes! Thank you, Dr. Kaufman. Thank you, Dr. Lipscomb."

"Beth."

"Yes, Dr. Lipscomb."

"This is your last semester of course work, isn't it?"

"Yes, it is."

"What are you planning to do for your dissertation?"

"I want to continue to study abuse among women."

"Do you have a chair for your study?"

"As a matter of fact, I don't."

"Interesting. Humm…. Think about what you want to do. Come see me, say next Tuesday, an hour before class."

The drive home was unusually short. I was traveling six feet off the ground! I didn't notice that the tree-lined streets of North Park were bursting with color. I didn't notice the children at the community center dressed in their football uniforms and large pads. I simply wanted to share the good news with Robert.

After driving into the garage, I hurried around the corner of the house and through the front door. Immediately upon entering the house, I noticed a heavenly scent of potatoes, cheese, broccoli and spices and followed the aroma to the kitchen. Robert had the table set and some homemade bread was on the table along with four dinner salads. In addition to the soup and mixed greens salad, he had included my favorite Middle Eastern appetizers: baba ghanouj, humus, creamed garlic, and tabouleh."

"How wonderful, Honey. You are always so wonderful. I can't wait to tell you my good news. Where are the boys?"

"They are down at Mrs. Blumfeld's house returning her pot. I confess. Mrs. Blumfeld made the soup and bread. I only picked up your favorite appetizers. I know you are working on something that means a lot to you, and I want to support you like you always support me."

Just then, Aaron and Jason entered the house. I called to them, "We are back here in the kitchen. Get washed up for supper. I want to hear all about your days."

Aaron talked about his college investigations and Jason talked about his new piano teacher's fame. They both discussed wanting to play basketball in the soon-to-start church league.

Then I shared my latest developments regarding school, my focus groups, and my therapeutic groups which will be supervised by the renowned Dr. Lipscomb.

After dinner the fellows took advantage of the remaining daylight and went to play basketball around the corner in the park while I cleaned the kitchen and went to thank Mrs. Blumfeld.

Mrs. Blumfeld's house was the only white brick colonial on the block. The entrance was recessed and presented a heavy carved crimson door. Matching crimson shutters were hung next to the windows. The three-car garage extended closer to the street than the entrance.

There was an absence of colorful flowers in her yard, but precision-cut shrubs and boulders made her landscape stunning. The door bell chimes reminded me of a chime I had heard in Frankenmuth. a little German theme town ninety minutes north of the Park."

"Mrs. Johnson, what a lovely surprise! Do come in."

The house was so welcoming, decorated as it was in deep red, chocolate browns and winter green.

"I want to thank you for the delicious soup and scrumptious bread, Mrs. Blumfeld."

"Jan...," she corrected me again. "Please call me Jan. Would you like some tea?"

"Tea would be lovely."

"Mrs. Johnson."

"Beth…. Call me Beth."

"Silly of me, Beth. I should be thanking you. I have spent years in this house shut away from the world, licking my wounds, feeling sorry for myself. I pushed away my daughter and friends until I did not know how to reach out to people.

"Then one day, I had one of my sick spells, after which you sent flowers and your family to visit me. Since then, I have begun to slowly come around again. You and your family were just what I needed when I needed it. Because of that, my dear, I must do the thanking."

"Jan, I see that you love the color red. I absolutely love red and so does my friend Estelle."

"Estelle Devereaux?"

"Why, yes. How might you know Estelle Devereaux?"

"When I was in the hospital, your husband said that he had run into some church members visiting someone across the hall from me. It was Estelle Devereaux. She introduced herself to me and-invited me to pray with her. She was most pleasant and shared with me how much you mean to her, my dear."

"Why, she never shared that with me."

"Oh, I am sure it was just an oversight."

"Well, Estelle's home is decorated in red and cream. I used reds, creams, yellow and black. I see that you have used red, browns and green. How interesting. I wonder if we have other things in common, Jan."

"Your husband tells me that you are an educator. I was a call-porter in order to put myself through college. Then I became a church school teacher, then public school social worker, then an assistant principal, and finally principal. I retired after 43 years of service.

"Now, I just sit at home not doing much at all. It's certainly been a pleasure to have your family and you visit with me. It was a pleasure to be able to share my cooking once again."

"But you are not well, Mrs. Blumfeld … I mean, Jan."

"A lonely heart can be worse than a congested and failing heart. Please accept what little help I can give. Your husband tells me that you are back in school."

"Why yes, I am."

"Well, a little help here and there can't possibly hurt."

"I'm sorry, I understand. But you must make me two promises. The first promise is that you will allow my family to help you, Mrs. Blumfeld. The second promise is that you must never ever become tired on our behalf."

"Beth, you have a deal."

After returning home, we watched a little television, discussed our daily lesson study and prepared for bed.

Usually, I would lie in bed thinking of all the wonderful blessings of the day. But, this evening I went to sleep right away.

Chapter 8 – The Dream

It was three thirty in the morning when Warmouth flew over the quiet streets of North Park, crash landing into the Spiritual Book and Gift Shop. Although the local bars, or watering holes, as they are called by the old folks, were closed, he was late for his 3 o'clock meeting with his company of demons.

Being late was unusual for Warmouth; but, tonight he had made it his special point to oversee nineteen-year-old Kennedy Mason's loss of virginity. Kennedy had met Milton three months earlier. Since then, Milton, a deacon at the Ebenezer Street Church, supplied her with money for her hair, clothes and nails. He never failed to flatter her, telling her how gorgeous she was.

He frequented the popular bar, the 'Hole in the Wall,' as a part of his job. He was a happily married police officer whose job was working vice. Girls like Kennedy helped him to keep his cover and satisfied his passion for the things his wife would not do in the privacy of their bedroom. Now in the back seat of his Cadillac Escalade, she found herself surrendering to his desire for her young, milky, curvaceous body.

Overcome by the passion of the moment, Kennedy's fully developed body shivered in lustful passion as she suppressed not only the cautions of her grandma Nana, but also the yearnings of the Holy Spirit to remain chaste. Grandma Nana had taught Kennedy not to make the same mistake her mother, Renée, had made. Renée became pregnant with Kennedy at the age of sixteen. Because of the closeness of their ages, Kennedy and Renée were more like sisters than mother and daughter. In fact, Renée and Kennedy were both raised by Renée's mother, Nana.

Grandma Nana, now a church-going woman, taught Kennedy lessons about Jesus and about Biblical character like Jacob, Ruth, Daniel, and Dorcas. She taught Kennedy all about

Paul and his writings on spiritual gifts. Grandma had even taught Kennedy to recognize her own spiritual gifts. Some late nights Kennedy would lie across Grandma Nana's bed, and they would talk about living a life of purpose, a life dedicated to God. Huddled under the covers in a bed that sank in the middle from being decades old, they would often discuss the importance of staying pure for marriage.

Although not fully developed, Kennedy's gifts were healing, exhortation, and prophecy. The gifts of healing and exhortation were tolerable; but, the most threatening to—the unseen onlookers was her gift of prophecy.

If her gifts were to mature, she could potentially pose too much of a threat to the dark principalities of this world. The forces of darkness could suffer serious injury if she were left to the guidance of the Holy Spirit. Besides, a spiritual curse had been placed upon her family before Kennedy was conceived, and it was time for those sins to visit Kennedy, a nineteen year-old nursing student. Some demon's head would roll because of this oversight.

Renée, her mother, had been sixteen when she got pregnant. Kennedy should have been pregnant by the age of fifteen. Because of Kennedy's faithfulness, the demons of lust had not been able to collect on Kennedy's generational curse. That is, not, until now.

It was utterly inexcusable for the Lust Division to make such oversights. With all their trying, they had failed to wear Kennedy down. Warmouth could not let this opportunity pass. The imp assigned to her detail had informed Warmouth that she was in full ovulation. This was an opportunity to stop her from breaking the curse. If he could manage to introduce an unwed pregnancy into her life, it would cause her to drop out of school and lose honor in her church.

"Great! Warmouth thought. This would also strengthen the curse placed upon her family two decades ago. Finally, this dumb creature had given him the ammunition to discredit her before she could grow strong. Until now, she had been too prone to obedience. Until now, she had listened to reason and conscience. Leaving her innocence in place was far too dangerous.

Grinning, he thought *we have her now*. He summoned a couple of foot-soldiers from his Lust Division to oversee the completion of the job. They surrounded the Escalade and vocalized seducing phrases.

'Oh, yes baby. Give it to me! I'm a woman now. I'm beautiful. I'm irresistible! Fill my cup!"

Although Kennedy could not physically hear their suggestions, their siren song could be heard on a neuronal level through the conduction of her bones.

As she began to give in to their temptations, Warmouth's focus turned to the meeting he was now missing. Turning with bended knees to spring into the air, he commanded that the Lust foot soldiers keep watch so that no one disturbed the movements inside the Escalade.

By the time, Warmouth reached the company command post inside the Spiritual Book and Gift Shop, his personal assistant was receiving progress reports from the rank and file. Sergeant Disease and Illness and Sergeant Stress had just taken their seats. Although more than half of the reports were already given, Warmouth listened intently to each remaining report.

A demon with medals on the right side of his breast plate jumped to his feet saying, "The Division of Lust reporting, Sir. Sir, the high schools are under control; television viewing is at an all time high; and our desensitization tactics are in full force. We are doing fantastic with having women wear revealing clothing and develop their self worth based on what society suggests. We are hitting them on every front.

"We have increased the incidence of individuals thinking about responding to perversion approximately 34 percent in our radius. Our young men seldom respect their female counterparts; and, best of all; their female counterparts have confused demons of lust for what they consider to be justly deserved independence.

"We have managed to break down their family training and replace their family values with peer values – all while their parents are lusting for a more comfortable lifestyle.

"Child sacrifice is more popular today than when parents sacrificed their children to Baal for prosperity. It is even better because we have learned not to sacrifice the children in fiery furnaces, but to use them to raise-up an army of defiance. My Lord, we have done away with the ovens and have replaced them with high-end luxury cars and burdensome mortgages."

Sergeant Lust's report was met by cheers.

Next, another demon with medals on the right side of his breast plate jumped to his feet saying, "The Division of Greed reporting, Sir. Sir, the merchants have inflated the price of fuel by an additional 22 percent.

"We have been successful in influencing the advertising media and estimate that, as a result, consumer debt is up approximately 12 percent from this time last year [almost as much as the increase in the national debt]. Spending is simply out of control!

"In addition, we have managed to drive theft up 26 percent, partly as a result of increased unemployment. A secondary gain is that depression is up another 19 percent from the first of the year.

"The other day, we were most victorious when we managed to drive the area's most influential pastor so far into debt that his car was repossessed and his savings were garnisheed. The congregation does not know, yet. Our delusions of grandeur have been working; the pastor will soon have to tap into the church treasurer to support his lifestyle.

"In addition, we are encouraging an unnatural relationship between the pastor and the church treasurer. You know we always get several Christians to fall when we magnify the character flaws of their pastors.

"In fact, Sir, my company has targeted unscathed Christians in this area in hope that we can get them not to pay their tithes. At last, this would surely remove their shields of protection."

Another round of cheers went out to Sergeant Greed.

The mood in the room changed as Sergeant Anger stood to report. "Sergeant Anger reporting, Sir. Youth homicides are up 21 percent from this time last year. Drive-by shootings are easier to induce because of the effects of television and video games.

"The other day, a twenty-year-old walked up to a seventeen-year-old and a sixteen-year-old and blew their brains out at a gas station down on 7 Mile Road. Again, this was to our credit because it happened in our radius. Unfortunately, my soldiers could not get the entire station to blow up. There was obviously some prayer coverage on someone at the station."

A round of laughs went out as Sergeant Anger attempted to finish his report. The sound of thunder interrupted the laughs as Sergeant Anger scowled! "I am not finished, you imbeciles.

"Stressed-out husbands are turning on their wives. They are verbally abusive, emotionally abusive and physically abusive.

"Women, on the other hand, are misdirecting their anger. They are blaming the-other women for their husbands' weaknesses.

"We are constantly telling women what other women have. And, might I add, we are constantly telling them what they don't have. They are taking out their insecurities and anger on their female friends and their female counterparts. Do not be fooled, their anger may be more subtle than their husbands', but the damage is far more reaching."

"We have the children watching this so that they, too, will begin to act out and misdirect their anger. Boys watch and grow up to be physically abusive. Girls watch and also grow up to be abusive, too; except they call it relational aggression. What a joke!

"Nevertheless, whether boy or girl, it is all a double bonus for us.

"Females are internalizing their stress and suffering at earlier ages. This stress and suffering drive up their incidences of cancer, depression, cardiac arrest, and aging. Of course, this is all the work of my demons.

"Hey! check this out. Many of these dumb bimbos are suffering from Post Traumatic Stress Disorder and are too dumb to realize this. We just keep piling on the stressors. By the time we finish with them, they have unexplained stomach problems, back-aches, sleep problems, head-aches and over react to emotional stimuli.

"Now, the report on my imp patrol detail. My imps are watching for those who suffer shame. Shame is a wonderful thing because we exploit shame. We torment those poor souls with who suffer shame. We take shame and make it so unbearable that our victims will take their own lives, escape through drugs, reenact their victimization, or take on anger as a defense mechanism.

"While these idiots are so conditioned to a right or wrong choice, we don't offer a right or wrong choice. We present many wicked choices. Whatever they choose, as long as it's not from the other side, we have them!

"Now you can cheer you idiots!"

Another round of cheers went out to Anger.

All eyes turned to Sergeant Control, because Sergeant Anger was always a hard act to follow. Sergeant Control stood, confidently playing his best hand first.

"Yes, my Lord. Sergeant Control reporting, Sir. My master piece of deception has been proven through the last two decades. Although a young tool, it is more effective than most I've used. We have wormed our way into the unconscious minds of the holy children of God. Our witchcraft, control, has been intermingled with self-righteousness. They are so consumed with prophecy, quoting scriptures, and judging each other, they can't see the beams, or shall I say, demons in their eyes. The fools are dripping in holiness and are on their way to hell.

"Sir, our queen bees are holding down the fort, although I believe our efforts have been dampened by some prayer coverage. But, trust me; we are looking for the praying ones. We will certainly keep them busy with trials and tribulations if we are allowed to do so.

"Anyway, I have strategically placed one or two queen bees at every church in the area to maintain control of women and to assassinate women who might otherwise cause us problems. My demons are on the lookout for women who are on target for one of the following: evangelism, exercising their spiritual gifts, successfully encouraging their children to pursue the special purpose to which they are called, and those who have discovered their purpose in life.

"We cause dissention and intimidation to fall upon these women of God. Our secret agents continuously listen to our prompts to bring up past mistakes, exclude our targeted women, betray each other, and gossip to bring about death of opportunities and eventually the death of their souls. Our queens' victims either give in to them, therefore making our queens their idol gods; or become anger and are then turned over to the spirits or, shall I say, soldiers under Sergeant Anger."

Just then, lightening flashed and the hosts trembled. Warmouth flicked his wing against the form taken on by Control and sent him flying outside the Gift Shop. Control regained his composure and returned in less than two second.

"Sergeant Anger," said Warmouth "You will not refer to us as spirits. We are soldiers or demons. Is that understood? Another reference to our past and I will personally demote you to an imp and assign you to one single soul."

"But Lord!....."

"Silence! Who is next?"

"Sergeant Jealousy reporting, Sir. Lord, I can handle my company and Sergeant Control's company if the need arises, Sir."

(Sniggles and giggles from the other soldiers)

Warmouth's wings slowed their flapping pace as he smiled and spoke to his favorite demon, "Sergeant Jealousy, you take your work seriously; however, you need not waste your jealously on a fellow soldier. Continue."

"Well, Sir. We have managed to cause inhabitants in our radius to look outside themselves and compare themselves to one another. We have caused them to focus on the gifts of others and not to see or understand their own gifts. Basically, their focus has become external rather than internal.

"We have taught them that someone can take what is yours and, not to trust the Source of their gifts. We have been especially successful with the women in the workplace, churches and organizations. We continuously whisper surmising and nasty little suggestions in their ears. We have them so messed up they don't know what hit them. They wrestle daily with us until they deny the power of God inside them. In order to do this, we have worked in close collaboration with the Insecurity Unit."

At that, Sergeant Jealousy spun around and gave Sergeant Insecurity a high-five! Then, high-fives were given all along the room.

"Sergeant Insecurity reporting, Sir. As reported by Sergeant Jealousy, our units are working closely together, Sir. Whereas Jealousy focuses on external thoughts, my unit zeroes in on internal thoughts. We destroy self-esteem by torments of doubt and stagnation. We tell our targets that they do not have gifts and that no one wants them. Best yet, we work to erase the discernment of why they were created. They do not trust that they can possibly have a purpose. They are so afraid of their insecurities being discovered, that they have begun to deflect their short-comings by sabotaging others. Our victims identify with jobs, positions, and power because they can't see their own worth.

"We have productively infiltrated churches too. We have especially targeted church officials. We have elders acting on their insecurities in the pulpit. They abuse their pulpits for popular and political gain. They even turn members against each other instead of preaching what was given to them.

"First elders are becoming ineffective because they are nurturing the insecurities of their pastors. They no longer tenderly point out their flaws. They are identifying with their positions and are afraid of losing rank.

"We have department heads fighting each other for power and position. We have betrayal, sexual favors, and office politics fully engaged. We have successfully infected 90 percent of the churches and offices in our radius, Sir."

Just then, Warmouth stood and silence feel upon the room as the soldiers waited his judgment.

"Men I want to first commend you on your hard work. Second, I want to encourage you to work fast and effectively; we have but a short time. Remember the generational curses we have placed. Do not let soldiers of the righteous help the Selfish One break our curses. These curses help us by providing habitual and genetic strongholds on these imbeciles.

"Third, we are to have a special guest tonight who will lay out a plan that is designed to make our efforts more effective. We are to place our energies on a specific target population and maintain the rest. So, it is with my great pleasure that I introduce a dynamic Two Star General. Let us welcome General Zaren Orenda Bubzabel."

Just then, flashes of lightening and rumbles of thunder shook the sky as General Zaren Orenda Bubzabel appeared. Upon arriving, he quickly changed into the form of an angel with eight black wings and feet of fire. He was bringing an important message from the Headquarters of Darkness.

"Thank you, soldiers. I have listened to the reports of your sergeants and I am pleased at your progress. In fact, I am here to not just lay out a plan; but, also to tell you that if you continue on your present course, your Commander Warmouth will be promoted to a first-star general.

"Need I remind you that the Prince of Darkness, the head of this great army, has a first line composed of a large company of four star generals. Four star generals have mostly political duties and handle heads of states and world movements. Together, these four star generals, make up a cartel focusing on the downfall of mankind on a global level.

"Three star generals coordinate the worlds' famine and disaster details. Two star generals are in charge of regions and countries. And one-star generals are in charge of major cities. If Commander Warmouth receives the promotion, he will be in charge of this sinful city and its metropolitan area. This means you stand a strong chance in being promoted."

Cheers were heard among demons in all the other cities in the metropolitan area as the demons in the Spiritual Gift and Book Store, known as Company D7, raised their voices to General Bubzabel's news.

He continued in a deep rumbling voice.

"Accolades from the Prince of this World: I stand before you today to lay out a new plan which attacks the inhabitants' natural weaknesses. Our time is short so listen closely. It is called: Operation Tongue. I know what you are thinking. We have used the poison of the tongue for centuries. It is one of our most successful weapons; but, we are introducing two new operations in this area: Mistrust and Mislead. Our target areas are those who are covered by prayer and those Christians whom we don't already have.

"There are many inhabitants, including some in this area, who have not fully committed to the other side. For these individuals, we want to destroy their shields of prayer and impede their prayer life. This means also targeting those praying for them. Make them believe that they should stop praying for those sinners. Tell them that they will never change. When the prayers stop, we will be free to make our moves.

"Next, we will attack the Christians who we don't already have. Don't bother with those who think they are saved, but are not. We will just use them to annoy the saved Christians and to make them lose faith.

"Have them start rumors, threaten to kick them off committees, don't invite them to parties and functions, make our people angry at them for telling the truth and make it seem as if the world has more civilized people than those inside churches.

"Tempt them to stay at home and not go to church. At first, have them watch a video or DVD of church. After they are comfortable not going to church; have others to invite them to secular functions instead of going to church. If that doesn't work, have our people call them and discuss secular things.

"Make them overeat so that they cannot hear the voice of God. Fill them with empty calories and play with them through food. Bounce them up and down like a yoyo chemically through food and drink. Encourage them to eat large meals after they have heard penetrating sermons.

"Fill their lives with stressors, and encourage them not to trust in the righteous One. They will be so agitated, sleepy and sluggish that God will not be able to reach them. In short, I want the tongues to murder, the world to be envied, temperance to be mocked, and physiological instability to interfere with sanctification.

"This will take careful synchrony by all of our companies. I am going to a meeting in a week or two with Warmouth and other generals. When Commander Warmouth returns, he will be able to give details that are more specific on our newer tactics. Until then, do your best.

"Companies Anger and Control will keep confusion going. Companies Jealousy and Insecurity will breed lack of confidence and attack everyone who seems to be focused on purpose. Keep them from trusting each other. Don't tempt them with bold lies; remember that misleading is a far better lie. The more subtle the lie, the more effective; and the more subtle your attack, the more effective your attack.

"Use the most subtle attacks with women especially. They have a natural sense of weakness for subtle assaults; so be very, very subtle. They are dumb and emotionally driven; they respond far quicker than they think."

The soldiers began to dance with glee. "We've got them now, baby," shouted Warmouth!

Chapter 9 – The Interpretation

The phone rang and I stretched my arm from beneath the sheets and picked up the receiver.

"Hello."

"Good morning, Beth, how was your day yesterday?"

"My Lord!" It was 5:45 a.m. and I was still sleeping. "I'm sorry. Good morning, Frank. How was your day yesterday?"

Frank gave his usual reply, "Pretty good. I can't complain."

"Frank, I was having a pretty weird dream just now. Satanic forces were having a meeting about how they operate. Wow! I think what was most interesting was that much of what I dreamed was about how women fall prey to the forces of darkness. They were introducing a plan called 'Operation Tongue.'

"Operation Tongue?"

"Yeah."

"I see what you are dealing with, Beth. Open your Bible to James 3. Read verses 2 through 12."

"Frank, I have a Message Bible up here this morning.

"Beth it doesn't matter; just read it."

> James 3:2 We get it wrong nearly every time we open our mouths. If you could find someone whose speech was perfectly true, you'd have a perfect person, in perfect control of life.
>
> 3 A bit in the mouth of a horse controls the whole horse. A small rudder on a huge ship in the hands of a skilled captain sets a course in the face of the strongest winds. A word out of your mouth may seem of no account, but it can accomplish nearly anything – or destroy it!
>
> 5 It only takes a spark, remember, to set off a forest fire. A careless or wrongly placed word out of

your mouth can do that. By our speech we can ruin
the world, turn harmony to chaos, throw mud on a
reputation, send the whole world up in smoke and go
up in smoke with it, smoke right from the pit of hell.

7 This is scary: You can tame a tiger, but you can't
tame a tongue—it's never been done. The tongue runs
wild, a wanton killer. With our tongues we bless God,
our Father; with the same tongues we curse the very
men and women he made in his image. Curses and
blessings come out of the same mouth!

10 My friends, this can't go on. A spring doesn't
gush fresh water one day and brackish the next, does
it? Apple trees don't bear strawberries, do they?
Raspberry bushes don't bear apples, do they? You're
not going to dip into a polluted mud hole and get a
cup of clear, cool water, are you?

"Now read verses 17 and 18 of the same chapter," Frank
said.

James 3:17 Real wisdom, God's wisdom, begins
with a holy life and is characterized by getting along
with others. It is gentle and reasonable, overflowing
with mercy and blessings, not hot one day and cold
the next, not two-faced. You can develop a healthy,
robust community that lives right with God and
enjoys its results only if you do the hard work of
getting along with each other, treating each other with
dignity and honor.

"Now read Romans 3:10 through 18."

10 As it is written, There is no one righteous, not
even one;

11 there is no one who understands, no one who
seeks God.

12 All have turned away, they have together
become worthless; there is no one who does good,
not even one.

13 Their throats are open graves; their tongues
practice deceit. The poison of vipers is on their lips
14 Their mouths are full of cursing and bitterness.
15 Their feet are swift to shed blood;
16 ruin and misery mark their ways,
17 and the way of peace they do not know.
18 There is no fear of God before *their eyes*.

"Wow, Frank this is so unreal; the word actually said poison and the demons used the word poison, too. This is my conviction exactly! I watch what females do to each other and I can't rest until I do something that makes some sort of difference in this area.

"I am more passionate about this than most anything. But talking about other females is so juicy. Sometimes I think we are addicted to the adrenaline it produces. We must produce endorphins when we really get going with the mess we keep up sometimes. Its origin may be in our sinful natures, but according to my dream, the forces of darkness get much mileage on how we are.

"It sounds like we have to rely on God to conquer the poisonous things in our mouths as well as the dreadful things we do."

Frank agreed, "That is correct, Beth. Well, we'd better pray. My next partner will be calling soon. Whose turn is it to pray?"

"It's my turn. What are your requests?"

"Let us pray for the sick among us. Pray that I not tire of well-doing. Let us pray for my prison ministry and for mid-week prayer meeting.

To Frank's list, I added, "I'd like to pray for understanding about how women treat each other. I'd also like to ask that God be with my friend Estelle. She's not looking great. Then we can pray for our usual. Hold on while I get on my knees."

"Are you ready?"

" Yes. Most kind and gracious Heavenly Father, we thank you for this new day. We thank you for being a God who is powerful, merciful and all knowing. We thank you for being a God who cares about our concerns and wishes. We thank you for being Holy. We thank you for being fair. We thank you for providing a robe of righteousness for us that we may be called your son and your daughter. We thank you for your many, many promises that you have gifted us with. We thank you for the hugs and kisses that our spouses and families provide.

"We humbly kneel before you, claiming your promise that if we ask, you will grant our wishes according to your riches in glory.

"Father God, in the name of your son Jesus, we ask that you will be with the sick among us. O Jehovah-rapha. We pray for physical, emotional, and spiritual deliverance for them, Father. We pray that their needs be met and that those about them will not forget to minister to them. Be with Estelle, Lord. She doesn't look great. Please meet her needs.

"I pray for my prayer partner, Lord. He has been so faithful in his different ministries, but he is only human. Please allow your Spirit to continue to rest upon him, giving him wings like an eagle. Let him not tire of well-doing. Give him the stamina he needs to be a faithful soldier for you. Let him be a workman that need not be ashamed and one who rightly divides your word. We thank you in advance for answering this prayer.

"We thank you for being with his prison ministry and we ask that you will continue to soften the hearts of the inmates until they accept you as their personal savior. Then, Lord, when they are released from prison, please have a support system in place so that their commitment to you may be sustained.

"Now, Father God, we ask that you will be with all those who will deliver your word during the mid-week prayer services; may the power of the Holy Spirit rest upon them that they may be your instruments in drawing men and women to you.

"Then, Father God, we ask that you be with our children. Please protect them, Lord. Shield them under your wing, and help them to have a personal relationship with you. Keep their feet from mischief and make success a personal friend to them.

"Help us to be the parents that you would have us to be.

"Now Lord, I especially ask that you would reveal your purpose for my life. Father, it appears that I enjoy studying the subculture of women. If this is the avenue for me to pursue; please let me know.

"Now, Lord, we ask that the words of our mouths and the meditations of our hearts be acceptable in Your sight, O Lord, our strength and redeemer. We ask these things in the name of the Father, and the Son, and the Holy Ghost, Amen.

"Frank, you have a beautiful day."

"You, too, Beth. Goodbye now."

Chapter 10 – Two Birds, One Stone

The day was ordinary. I could not; however, forget the dream I had had during the night. Mr. Williams knocked at the door to my classroom to empty the trash. I enjoyed Mr. Williams; he reminded me of my father who had died some twenty-five years earlier.

"My father, Ed Garner, a hard working man, had been a building superintendent. He worked for the city during the day, but worked five evenings a week as a janitor so that his family would have the extra comforts he dreamed of having when he was a child. He was never too proud to do honest work. He was especially proud that I went to college. Dad had been a straight "A" student who quit school in the grade eight because he only had two pairs of pants and was totally was responsible for his own care.

"Hello, Mr. Williams. How are you today?"

Doing a holy dance, he responded, "Saved, sanctified and washed in the blood of the Lamb. Have mercy! Thank you, Jesus! How are you, Mrs. Johnson?"

"I am thankful to be alive and more thankful that God has blessed my family."

"So, Mrs. Johnson, when are you going to walk in your gift?"

"Okay, Mr. Williams. Everything was fine until you started that gift 'thang' again. Are you 'walkin' in *your* gift?"

"Why don't you and your husband come and visit my church? Services start at 10:30 every Sunday. Oh! Before I forget, the Mrs. sent you some of her famous peanut brittle. I will bring you the package later today."

"Why thank you, Mr. Williams. I love peanut brittle."

When the door closed, I shook my head, thinking of the suggestion that I would have the gift that Mr. Williams suggested. Why, I couldn't even form my mouth to say such foolishness.

Oh my, where had the morning gone? It was time for lunch and I still had not contacted Human Resources to request a leave of absence form. Mrs. Kolinsky and Mrs. Jones were already eating when I pulled the nuked remnants of my left-over dinner out of the microwave.

The afternoon was ordinary. Eileen was regaining more memory and was beginning to show some restraints in judgment. Carlos Burns returned to school after his parole officer threatened to lock him up for truancy. Kim Weatherspoon demonstrated that she had reached all of her goals and was showing evidence that she was using her skills outside of school.

As I reached for my sweater, Mr. Williams knocked on my office door. "I'm glad I caught you, Mrs. Johnson. Here is that peanut brittle I promised you."

"Thank you, Mr. Williams. This is right on time because I have to make a stop before I get home. You and Mrs. Williams are angels." I waved goodbye and headed for the University.

Upon reaching the elevator, a voice rang out, "Hold the elevator for me, Beth." It was Mary Mathews. Mary was one of the nicest women I'd ever met. She was studying sociology at the University and although in a different program, we took some classes together.

"Mary, I was thinking of you the other day. Dr. Lipscomb is supervising an independent study of mine and asked me to think about a co-facilitator for a group I want to conduct. Would you be interested in hearing about the project?"

"I would if I can use this as clinical time. I will be writing Comprehensives in December. What about you?"

The elevator door opened.

"Great! I plan to write in June. I am just about to go to Dr. Lipscomb's office to discuss the group. Can we talk about this later after class?"

"Sure let's I have something to take care of now. Later will be great."

As her door was open, I announced, "Hello, Dr. Lipscomb, I am here for our meeting about the encounter group. May I come in?"

"Sure, I am just finishing up a correspondence and I will be right with you. Have a seat."

After a few more key strokes, Dr. Lipscomb turned to me and said, "Okay Beth that ought to do it. Listen, your work on the women's focus group on abuse is most interesting. As I recall, you are nearing the dissertation phase."

"Yes, I am. I really want to further investigate the interactions of women. I find this topic intriguing and, as I shared with you and Dr. Kaufman, the women in the focus group would like to continue working as a group. I told them that there was a possibility that we could begin a therapeutic or encounter group. The only thing is that the holidays are upon us and the holidays are not a good time for meetings or starting anything new."

"Then start your group the first of the year, but send out announcements throughout the holidays. What I need from you is a write-up on the members of your new group. You can code their names for the purpose of confidentiality.

"Next, I will need for you to choose a co-facilitator. Then you will need to screen each member to ensure that they are mentally healthy enough to participate in a group. No psychosis or that sort of thing. Last, you need to reserve a meeting room before the end of this semester."

"Those things are doable. In fact, I was thinking about Mary Mathews for my co-facilitator."

"Mary Mathews? I don't think I know the name."

"She is a doctoral student in the Sociology Department who is also ready to take her comprehensive examinations at the end of this semester. She is working on birth order and families of origin with victims of abuse in her dissertation proposal. She needs clinical hours."

"What will be the focus of your dissertation proposal?"

"I want to look at how women perceive abuse or mistreatment among themselves.

"May Mary and I can do the group together; yet, conduct our separate studies simultaneously."

Dr. Lipscomb responded, "Your focuses would have to differ. For example if you focus on women's interactions, Mary might want to focus on families of origin. I would expect two different sets of progress notes, one from you and one from Mary after each session. Talk with Mary and ask her to come see me. If we agree, I will call her advisor to ask permission."

* * *

"Hey, Mary. I talked with Dr. Lipscomb and she spoke very positively about the possibility of our conducting a group together. She wants separate progress notes and a separate focus for each of us. She's expecting you to talk with her and then to your advisor. Perhaps our departments can collaborate. Let's go to the student union, have a cup of tea and some peanut brittle, and discuss the details."

"Sure, I love peanut brittle."

We had a very productive [and enjoyable] two-hour meeting where we roughed out the general outline of our joint project.

Pushing back her chair, signaling the completion of the meeting, Mary summarized, "Now let me see if I clearly understand. We will do brief group encounters of a therapeutic nature. During these encounters, you will focus on the interactions between women and I will focus on understanding the family of origin dynamics.

"We will work together as co-facilitators and turn in separate summaries of how we processed the information gleamed from each group. Your progress notes will focus on the interactions between women. My progress notes will focus on the families of origin dynamics.

"We can do combined progress notes as long as both areas are covered. But in the end, we must do separate overall reports."

"Exactly!" I agreed.

"Great. I am sure my advisor won't have a problem with this."

Upon reaching home, I told Robert all about my day and the meetings with Dr. Lipscomb and Mary Mathews. My concern was finding extra time to study for comprehensives and also plan the group therapy with the year-end holidays approaching. Like always, Robert smiled and said, "You will get it done."

Chapter 11 – The Preparation

Robert was right. By sacrificing a few hours of shuteye each week, I pulled it together. As I had promised, I sent the following letter to the members of the original groups:

November 13

Dear Ladies,

Our focus groups this past October were very successful. I personally thank each of you for your participation. I was able to learn much from you and would, as discussed, like to continue to learn more about the interactions between women.

As you requested, I have decided to offer a therapeutic encounter group in order to examine the interactions between women and take a look at their families of origin.

I am extending an invitation to women from all three focus groups to participate in a therapeutic group in January next year. A separate invitation will also be sent to some churches and local businesses. If you are interested, please phone me on my cell phone, (313) 555-5293, email me, or return the enclosure completely filled out so that we may conduct a brief interview required for admittance into the group.

When conducting a group of 8 to 12 women, it is customary that two co-facilitators manage the group. My co-facilitator is Mary Mathews. She is a doctoral student in the Department of Sociology at the University and is very capable. I am sure that the group will just love her.

The group will meet weekly for approximately 10 weeks. Each session will last 90 minutes. It is important that no session is missed. In cases of extreme emergency, however, you may miss one session without having to drop out of the group. Once the group begins, no other member will be admitted.

The group will be limited to the first 12 women to respond and qualify. So, an early response is advised. Interviews will begin December 4 and last through December 7. Mary will conduct interviews from 10 a.m. until 3 p.m. I will conduct interviews on the same days from 4 p.m. until 9 p.m.

The interviews will take place in conference room C on the 3rd floor in the Southfield Public Library. Each person interviewed will be contacted within five business days with a decision regarding your qualification for the group. The group will begin on January 11

After the interviews, Mary sent me an email:

December 11

Dear Beth,

I think the interviews went well. I was amazed that so many women wanted to get into the group. I am bouncing this acceptance notice to you for your approval. Please look it over one last time before I mail them.

I suggest we mail acceptance letters tomorrow and reminder letters at the first of January. Perhaps you can make phone calls two days before to remind women of the starting date and time.

By the way, did you write your comprehensive examinations?

Mary Mathews

email response to MMathews@yahoo.com

Or mail to

City University Educational Psychology and
Community Counseling Departments
1373 Cass Avenue
Detroit, Michigan 48203
313 577-2323

December 15, 2000

Congratulations Felicia Terrell,

You have been selected to be a group member in the Women's Encounter and Therapeutic Group.

Featuring: Women's Abuse Issues
Where: 3rd floor Conference Room
University Education Building
When: January 11
Time: 5:30 p.m. to 7:00 p.m.
Facilitators: Mary Mathews, Doctoral Candidate
Beth Johnson, Doctoral Student

Mary was right on, so I emailed her back:

December 17

Dear Mary,

The letter looks great! Let's do it. My comprehensives are this June. Still, knowing that I am in school, my husband and the kids were very supportive and my sister and friends, Estelle and Jan, pitched in and helped with the holiday cooking and the clean-up. How were your comprehensives?

Oh, I almost forgot. Good news! My leave of absence was approved for one year, so I will have time to really concentrate.

Respond to: BethJohnson@sbcglobal.net

PS: I have attached the brief profiles of all the women in the group. They will be sent to Dr. Lipscomb so that she may review our decisions before the beginning of the next semester.

ATTACHMENT:

Felicia Terrell is a 56-year-old woman who was married 22 years. Her former husband divorced her for a woman 20 years her junior. Four of her five children are out of the house, leaving one 17-year-old female, and two business partners living in her home.

Felicia is a contractor who builds decks and additions, along with other improvements to single-family homes.

She speaks softly, does not speak much and appears to have a Type B personality. Her highest level of education is trade school where she earned an Associate's Degree. She has one female friend. Felicia was a part of one of the focus groups conducted by Beth Johnson. The interviewer was Beth Johnson.

Elisa Nixon is 51 years old. She is twice divorced. The first divorce was from a man who was physically abusive. The second divorce was cited as "something that just happened."

Her spiritual orientation is that of being anti-dogmatic. She resists organized religion, especially when rules are imposed upon her. She is the second of two children and has an older brother. Her parents are hard-working and entrepreneurial in nature. She has a Type A personality and appears driven for success. At times, she appears agitated. There are other times when she appears delightfully sassy. Participant speaks of having close female friends; however, when questioned, she says she spends little time with them. Elisa was a part of one of the focus groups conducted by Beth Johnson. The interviewer was Beth Johnson.

Penny King is a 49-year-old school administrator who is married to a professional man who is seven years her junior. Together they have three children, two daughters and one son. All her children attend her school. The couple has strong Christian beliefs and is extremely active in their church. Penny married her husband in her mid thirties. She states she is accustomed to getting what she wants and says that she is not manipulative.

Penny is from the Bronx where she attended a large church which she warmly refers to as The Blessed Brotherhood of the Bronx. Penny, her brother, and their mother are said to be natural leaders. Her older brother is a plastic surgeon, and her younger sister has cerebral palsy. Penny was a part of one of the focus groups conducted by Beth Johnson. The interviewer was Mary Mathews.

Melanie Robinson is a 29-year old single female with three daughters, ages 11, 12, and 14. She has never been married. Developmental milestone are reported within normal range, physically. She seems to have emotional scars stemming from her relationship with her mother and her mother's boyfriends. Still, she appears to be stable.

She is the older of two sisters. She seems to perceive friendship quickly, demonstrates a sanguine personality type and a dependent personality. She appears not to be highly intuitive. Melanie was a part of one of the focus groups conducted by Beth Johnson. The interviewer was Beth Johnson.

Madison Gathers is a 49-year-old woman married to a charismatic minister. She is the business manager of her husband's church and accompanying school. After attending one year of college, she dropped out to do ministry. Together they have five children: the eldest, 24; the youngest, eight. She appears docile, but claims to direct much of her husband's affairs. Their religious beliefs are very conservative. Both Madison and her husband come from a family of achievers.

She has plenty of friends and is the younger of two girls. Her older sister and uncles are attorneys. Her husband's brothers are also attorneys. She speaks softly and appears to be highly perceptive. Her mental status is judged as alert. Madison received an announcement about the focus group at her church. Madison was not a part of any previous focus group of this nature. The interviewer was Beth Johnson.

Dorothy Scott is a 56-year old who bore one daughter. Her daughter's father lived between Dorothy's home and the home he provided for his wife. Although not married to him, Dorothy reports that she has spent much of her life 'pining' over him. After the relationship was over and her daughter had left for college, Dorothy began corresponding with a prisoner. She married him after six months of visits and letter writing.

She is now heavily involved in her church where she runs a flower, book and gift shop. At times, her affect was depressed. However, she uses humor to cheer herself. Dorothy was a member of one of the focus groups conducted by Beth Johnson. The interviewer was Beth Johnson.

Wilma Bryant is a 27-year-old single woman who was recently baptized. She came to the group after discussing reading an ad for the encounter group in her church bulletin. After sharing with her new first lady that she was a member the first focus group on mistreatment among women, they decided to apply to the group. Wilma reported finding comfort in the support of first lady Madison Gathers. She has been experiencing some personal conflicts with relationships and thought that she would gain the wisdom she needed to make some important decisions. She presented with normal affect. She is an only child.

Wilma was not a part of any previous focus group of this nature. The interviewer was Mary Mathews.

Bertha Harvey is a 39-year-old former minister's wife. She is presently married to a police officer. She had two daughters by her first marriage and two sons by her second. She is a charter school teacher in the area of special education. She presents as spiritually grounded and realistic. She is the middle child in a family of three girls. According to Bertha, her mother has a similar disposition as she; and her father is a jovial ladies' man.

Bertha was a part of one of the focus groups. Interviewer: Mary Mathews.

Sue Gaston is a 39-year-old married woman who works as an office manager at a local business. Sue heard about the focus group from her prayer partner and decided to schedule a morning interview. She had recently become chronically ill and thought she needed to express her feelings in a safe environment.

Although, Sue is not a member of a church, she has a flourishing prayer life with her prayer partner. Sue is the eldest of four children. She was not a part of any previous focus group of this nature. Sue was interviewed by Mary Mathews.

Allyson Akins is a 39-year-old single female student at the University. She is completing her Master's in social work and is Women Ministries Leader at her church. She is engaged to marry and appears passionate about life. Allyson received notice of the group through the mail and has arranged to receive contact credit at the University for her participation in the group. Allyson was not a part of any previous focus group of this nature. The interviewer was Mary Mathews.

Renée Mason is a 36-year old who lives with her 53-year-old mother, 70-year-old great grandmother, and 19-year-old sister. She was raised to attend church; however, she stopped attending services around the age of sixteen. Renée reports being at a cross road in her life and feels stuck. She works in an automobile factory and is facing unemployment due to down-sizing. Renée was a part of one of the focus groups conducted by Beth Johnson. The interviewer was Mary Mathews.

Jasmine Rivers is a 42-year old homemaker from Ann Arbor. Jasmine states that she is from a wealthy family and spends much of her time reading, singing, traveling, and enjoying the outdoors. She presents calm and pleasant and states that joining this group will afford her the opportunity to interact with adult women. Jasmine was not a part of any previous focus group of this nature. The interviewer was Beth Johnson.

Psssst. Forming is easy. Although most groups go through the Forming, Norming, Storming and Performing stages, this was no ordinary group. Oh, dear! I've managed to keep quiet up to now; shame on me for giving you another peek.

Chapter 12 – The Group Session One: Forming

The holidays were behind us and January 11 was finally here. The women arrived. Small groups of two or three formed outside the conference room as they recognized others from their earlier focus groups. Some new members sat isolated in the scattered chairs. Mary was putting final touches on some packets of information. It was time.

I entered the waiting room area, thanked the group for coming, and invited the women to help themselves to the refreshments on the table in the conference room.

The room was furnished with a rich-looking mahogany conference table pushed against the south wall. We had assembled a circle of chairs no beginning and no end — in the middle of the room.

There were three large ceiling-to-floor windows covered by wooden horizontal blinds. On the side of each blind was a light brown fabric with a light blue, chocolate brown and taupe striped pattern. The fabric swooping across the top and hanging on the sides of the blinds touched the light brown carpet woven with varying shades of blue and taupe speckles.

Kissing the walls were cleverly matted prints displaying the motivational words: wisdom, dedication, forgiveness, joy, courage, and persistence. The aroma in the air was that of new carpet mixed with the allure of fresh brewed hazel-scented coffee, emanating from the rectangular shaped table against the north wall. Next to the coffee pot were two baskets, one with fresh fruit, the other with granola bars, candy bars, peanut butter crackers, and potato chips.

Mary moved to the south side of the circle, while I moved to the north and announced, "Ladies, if you would find a seat, we will begin."

Penny and Melanie moved to the right of Mary. Allyson and Elisa moved to the right of me.

"As many of you know, my name is Beth Johnson and I am a co-facilitator of this group. The other facilitator is Mary Mathews. Mary was not in the waiting area earlier because she was putting the final touches on some packets of information.

"We want you to know a little more about us. For example, Mary's therapeutic style is based on a therapist named Alfred Adler.

"Adler's style involved delving into the family of his clients and birth order in order to ascertain whether those dynamics may contain clues to help mobilize the client to higher levels of independence.

"On the other hand, I favor a style of therapy that is based on the relationship between the therapist and client, the client's perception of her purpose in life, and changing the way we think through reading and other types of work. This clinical style was developed by Carl Rogers and Rollo May.

"Although Mary and I have our favorite approaches, we prefer to think of ourselves as caring, sensitive clinicians who will draw from our experiences to provide whatever you need at the time you need it. You will find more information on our therapeutic styles in the packets that Mary placed on the table earlier. We want to make sure you are informed.

"There are coffee and snacks on the table behind me. Since we are meeting during the dinner hour, we hope that these snacks will tide you over until you are able to eat your supper. Feel free to grab a bite during the session. Next week, the conference room will be open thirty minutes early so that you can have a beverage and a snack before the session starts.

"Please help yourselves to anything on the table, or feel free to bring your own sandwich to eat before the session. I only ask that you place all trash in the containers outside the conference room."

Turning to Mary, I asked "Will you get us going this evening?"

"Thank you, Beth. My name is Mary Mathews. I am delighted that Beth asked me to co-facilitate this group. Before we get started, I want to go over three ground rules.

"Rule number one is honesty. One of the reasons you were selected to participate in the group is that you all expressed your willingness to be honest in this group process. During the course of these groups, we will be challenged not only to be honest with each other, but also to be honest with ourselves. Each of us will only get out of this process whatever we put into it.

"Rule number two is confidentiality. What is said in this room stays in this room. We need to all agree to this before we go any further." (*Heads nodded from the ladies in the group.*)

"Confidentiality is important so that we may all feel safe and free to actively participate. Confidentiality is important so that we are willing to be vulnerable enough to let others see who we are. We need confidentiality in order to express our deepest concerns.

"Do we have anyone who is concerned with confidentiality or about being able to keep secret the things said in this room?"

(Although the pause was only a minute, it felt like an eternity to Mary.)

"Great! Finally, rule number three: During the course of these sessions, we will roll up our sleeves and actively participate. We ask that each of you take the group seriously and attend every session. Missing one session due to an unavoidable emergency sometimes happens; however, if you miss more than one session, please check with Beth or me to see if you can continue.

"Beth, do you have any rules you wish to share?"

"Yes, Mary, I also have three rules. But, they are more like requests than rules.

"Request one is that we try to stay in the here-and-now. That means that, as best we can, let's talk about what is concerning us today. Occasionally, the need may arise to visit your past, so don't be thrown by this. The past isn't our focus, but we may ask you about your past.

"Request two is that we refrain from hurting one another. One way to do this is to talk about yourself by using *I* statements. For example, '*I* feel that *I* am not being understood,' instead of '*You* don't understand me.'

"My third and last request is that you take ownership in your progress. That means that you will decide what you want to accomplish as a group. Although you have a predetermined topic of *women's abuse issues*, there may be something specific you want to address.

"In order for a group of this nature to be successful, there must be an overall goal. We have stated that we plan to investigate the interactions among women and take a look at our families of origin. It is now your job to decide on one or two more specific goals for this encounter. Are there any questions?"

(Pause)

Since there were no questions, I suggested, "Perhaps you would like to start by introducing yourselves to each other and sharing why you decided to join this group."

Silence filled the room. Mary wondered who would emerge and take the early lead. I avoided making eye-contact with the ladies, so that I wouldn't thereby sanction a leader.

Allyson and Penny spoke-up at the same time. Allyson yielded.

"My name is Penny. I am a school administrator. I am told that women think that I am pushy and bossy. Women leaders get bad reputations when they do the same things that men leaders do. Men are considered wonderful, while I am considered aggressive for exerting strong leadership.

"I am referred to as a name I won't repeat, and I am ready to take a closer look at myself. So, I guess I would like to look at my leadership style."

When Penny completed her statement, the yielding lady chimed in, "My name is Allyson. Speaking from my experience as a student in the social work program and as Women's Ministries Director at my church, I have seen the effects of the meanness of women. Niki Crick, out of the University of Minnesota, called it *this meanness relational aggression.*

"I would like to come up with some ideas to teach women about what we do to each other. I heard that this group would focus on the same thing. I think that we can be leaders without mistreating other women."

The next lady indicated her desire for healing, "My name is Elisa and I would like to get over the hurt I have experienced as a result of the meanness of women. After I participated in an earlier focus group, I came to understand that what we do to each other is abusive."

Without hesitation, Melanie added, "My name is Melanie and I have personally experienced pain from the actions of other women. I would like for this group to help me figure out what I am doing to cause this type of treatment. Someone told me once that we are responsible for the way people treat us; and I find that hard to believe."

Madison's goal was stated very briefly, "Hello, I am Madison. I would like to learn more about myself."

That statement prompted another lady to say, "Hi, my name is Dorothy. I've done some not-so-nice things in my life; and I don't know why. Like Madison, I would like to learn more about myself."

This theme was continued by the next speaker, "Good evening, I am Renée. I feel as if I have made some bad decisions with the women in my life. I want to be more responsible. I don't know if I have personally tried to hurt other women. But, I think that I have caused some damage unknowingly. That's why I am here."

The next speaker informed us, "Hi, my name is Sue, and I am here because my prayer partner recommended this group. She has invited me to some of her game parties, but I have refused stating that I have trust issues with women. I don't know if these feelings are really trust issues with women or trust issues with my husband. I am confused.

"Well, one day my prayer partner, Estelle, told me about this group. So, here I am."

The next lady changed the direction a bit, "My name is Jasmine, and I am here for the opportunity to interact with adult women. I was in Crowley's Department Store; and I was humming this tune when Beth Johnson complimented me on my voice. I gave her a word, we talked, and she told me about this group."

The next lady was prompted by a previous speaker, "Hi, my name is Wilma and I am here with my new first lady, Madison. After I was baptized two months ago, I asked the pastor's wife if there were counseling services available. She told me about the ad for this group in the church bulletin. Ironically, I was a part of the focus group that led to this group. I am here because life is very confusing for me right now. I am experiencing drama and peace at the same time."

The last speaker was also an alumna of one of the focus groups. "Hello, my name is Felicia. I attended one of the focus groups. I am not proud of everything that I have done, and I am here because I am ready to take a look at some of my behavior."

Scanning the room and looking into the eyes of each woman one by one, I reassured them, "Your reasons for joining this group appear to be good reasons. Now, can you get together and turn these reasons into two or three goals for your group?"

Mary and I observed the interpersonal dynamics as the women began to clarify their goals. Penny took the lead by asking questions. Madison reached into her purse, pulled out a note pad and began to write. Felicia pulled her chair closer to Madison and began to help her remember all that she had heard. Allyson rephrased the responses of each woman to help them clarify their feelings. Elisa and Bertha asked probing questions. Madison appeared to study each woman.

Melanie turned away from the group to ask Mary if they were doing what was expected of them. Then, turning away from the group again, she told me how much she was enjoying the activity.

After about twenty minutes of discussion, Allyson read three goals. "Goal one: to understand aggression. Goal two: to understand why we treat each other badly. Goal three: to explore how to teach others how to treat us properly."

Mary congratulated the women on a job well done as I placed a chair in the middle of the circle. Standing behind the chair, I explained, "I want each of you to take turns sitting in this chair. While you are sitting in this chair, we ask that you sincerely do the following things:

"One: Briefly describe one of your most significant encounters with a woman that left you feeling good. Two: Briefly describe one of your most significant encounters with a woman that left you feeling badly."

Allyson stood, went over to the chair and sat in it. "Recently, I became engaged to a man named Marcus," she said. "Well, one day my future mother-in-law insisted on surprising me with her out-of-town company. They wanted to meet me and see my place. My future sister-in-law could not warn me because that day I had left my cell phone at home. So, she called my sister and told her what was going on. I got home around 8:00 p.m. and when I drove-up, Marcus's mom was getting out of her car with her company. I thought, 'Oh my goodness! I cannot believe it!'

"What I did not know was that earlier that day, my sister and future sister-in-law had gone into my apartment and cleaned everything. They left fresh flowers and wonderful air fresheners in a few places. To top all that, they bought some groceries and prepared some food.

"When I opened the door, everything was clean and there was a sealed note in an envelope on the counter that explained everything. I felt really good that they went through all of this trouble to make me look good. But, I also felt angry that my future mother-in-law was so inconsiderate."

Elisa took the chair, "The other day, the woman in my office who had undermined me before told me I should leave work early because I was looking poorly. She said that I should see a doctor. And, I was feeling horribly. Although she usually makes me feel badly by constantly harassing me, I felt good because she showed compassion."

Renée stood next and sat in the chair. "The other day I was at this really upscale night club. A woman passing by said to her friend that my weave looked like a slaughtered animal, and they laughed. I felt out of place and poor.

"Now on the other hand, the best thing that a woman has done for me is to raise my child. My mother raised Kennedy, the girl I refer to as my sister. I feel especially bad because I have not been a good example to my daughter."

Sue stood and walked to the chair. She was barely in the seat when she sputtered out, "My prayer partner Estelle takes so much time with me. She prays with me. She doesn't even know me, but she listens. Isn't that wonderful?

"I cannot think of anything a woman has done to make me feel really bad. Sorry."

Penny stood and walked to the chair. "I have felt worst when I felt betrayed by women. I feel best when they support me."

Madison went to the chair in the middle of the circle and added, "I feel badly when my sisters and uncles are talking about legal stuff and I can't join in on the conversation.

"I feel really good when women in our congregation compliment me for singing or taking care of business."

Dorothy sat in the chair and said, "I feel badly when people brag about how much they have, when I am scraping to get by. I feel good when I help others."

Melanie went to the chair. "I feel good when I get to laugh and talk with all the fancy ladies while doing their hair. I feel badly when those same women snub me when I am out at a function. Like, I do hair for this celebrity. She has always promised to introduce me to other celebrities. But, she breaks her promise all the time."

Bertha stood and went to the chair. "I feel badly after I yell at my daughter. I feel good when I spend time with my best friend."

Felicia went to the middle of the floor. "I feel good when I can be open and honest. I feel badly when I stop to think that my actions are hurting another woman."

Jasmine followed. "I feel badly when women judge me unfairly. I feel good when they take the time to get to know me."

Just then, Mary stood-up and announced, "Ladies, we are almost out of time. Remember, we will meet here next Thursday at the same time. We are also asking that you start a journal of your experiences in this group.

"We would like for you to write at least one page in your journal every time we have a group session. We would like for you to start by writing a reason or principle for the things that made you feel good and a reason for the things that made you feel bad. You have a worksheet in your packets that explains what we want you to do.

"One side of the page has the word 'good;' the other side has the word 'bad.' Think about all the things you have just heard and try to extract the principles behind the feelings. For example, one principle resulting in 'good' feelings might be compassion; while one principle resulting in 'bad' feelings might be inconsideration.

"I see that our time is up; so, we will see you next week. Don't forget your assignment."

Chapter 13 – Processing Session One

Obviously excited about Session One, I asked Mary, "How do you think that went?"

"It was great! I loved the goals they came up with. They appeared to be honest," exuded Mary.

"My sentiments exactly!"

Mary continued, "After we started, I wondered if it was a good idea to allow Madison and Wilma to be in the same group. It's tough enough for a pastor's wife to make friends and open up as it is; there seems to be an imbalance of authority there. We need to watch that."

How wonderful! We were on the same wave length. I concurred, "I was thinking the same thing during the session."

As Mary continued, I was glad I had chosen her to work with me. "It was also interesting that Penny and Melanie moved to my right and Allyson and Elisa moved to the right of you."

"It sure was, Mary. I noticed that your presentation was more authoritative – you know – in setting rules. My presentation was more maternal in that I stated my wishes as requests rather than rules. I think it might be possible that Penny identified with your authority and Melanie sought your approval.

"I gather that Melanie was seeking approval when she asked if the group was doing well. I would expect that from her family of origin. Allyson appeared to wear her intellectualism a bit strongly. I think she moved to my right because she identified with my work on abuse and women. And, perhaps, Elisa moved to my right because she has that mother issue going on as well. Anyway, our different styles could come in handy if issues with families of origin arise. Let's continue to function within our comfort zones."

"Did you notice how Penny took the lead? But, the question is, Will she keep the lead after they storm? Now, I was really floored when Renée said that she had a sister, Kennedy, who is really her daughter. That piece of history did not come up in the interview. That would make her grandmother, mother, and her each around 16 or 17 when they conceived.

"Hmm. Kennedy, Renée.... Why do those names sound so familiar?"

Mary reared back in her chair. "Wow! A family confession on the first night. I hope this is a sign of their comfort level."

"I think so. We really did not get into their families of origin tonight; perhaps you might want to think about just when you want to do this," I suggested. "It would be great information in the beginning of the sessions while they are in the *forming stages*, like session two or three. Or, you may want to wait until we need some psychoanalyses to trace the beginnings of behaviors. It's your call. I'm going to stick around to do my clinical notes while everything is fresh."

"Good idea. Then we can walk to the parking structure together and talk more. Of course, we can't use names."

Chapter 14 – Session Two: Prelude to the Storm

The heavy doors to the conference room were now shut. I smoothed my pants as I bent to sit in the same chair I had sat in during the previous week. "Okay, ladies let's begin. How many of you made an entry into your journals?" Seven hands shot up.

"Of course, we can't make you write in your journals; but we can share that it will really help you not only to process what is going on inside the group; but also to see your circumstances more clearly. Those words on your homework sheet can help you clarify your feelings. Trust me; the benefit is all yours.

"Last week you came up with three wonderful goals; so this week we would like to start with aggression. We have a one-page write-up on aggression. Would someone like to read it?"

Melanie raised her hand. The pamphlet was passed to her. She read with interest.

Mary jump-started processing the pamphlet, "So who wants to tell what they heard about aggression?"

Allyson: "I heard that aggression is a strong emotional energy which is useful only if it is channeled the right way. Melanie read that we all have some form of aggression, whether we act it out or not.

"Aggression can take on many forms if not channeled correctly, such as high blood pressure, heart strain, rapid heart beats, headaches, ulcers, skin rashes, panic attacks, stomach upsets, toothaches, and more."

Penny: "I heard that aggression is one of the main reason humans have survived for centuries. Aggression is useful. It helps us to overcome obstacles."

Bertha: "Yeah, but she also said that it is energy that does not leave your body, and it is only useful if channeled properly, like sports or work on creative hobbies and productive things.

Unfortunately, aggression is often used negatively – to lash out at innocent people, destroy something we worked hard to build, or put individuals or groups down."

Madison: "I think she also said that anger and competition are forms of aggression. But, isn't a little competition healthy?"

Jasmine: "I heard there is concern if you get into fights, push people away, or become angry when they stay away, mutter under your breath, are rough with pets and people, have temper tantrums and you can't keep friends."

Bertha: "She also read that when the underlining cause of your antagonism toward yourself and others is discovered, then your aggression can be reduced."

Beth: "Because we are discussing aggression – and anger and competition are forms of aggression, I am going to ask each of you to share two things. First, share what it is about women that angers you. Second, share circumstances where you have competed with another woman."

Penny: "Well, I am annoyed when women try to usurp my authority. Women are just like men. They try to knock you off the proverbial mountain. I find men more accepting than women. That bothers me. And as far as competition is concerned, I really don't compete with women. They compete with me."

Allyson: "I am annoyed when women are pushy and bossy. I find it offensive when women throw stones and hide their hands. They seem to manipulate by getting other people to do their dirty work – then pretend to be all innocent. I think I am more aggressive toward that type of woman. Yet, I am not sure if I am competing with them or am only bothered by them."

Melanie: "I am bothered by women who judge. I think I compete with women to show the world that I am as normal as other women."

Bertha: "I am angered by women who blindly do the bidding for men who are controlling. For example, I have a friend who divorced her husband, a 'trusted' member of a congregation. The women in the congregation told my friend that she was going to hell. Never mind the fact that he beat her for sport. They actually took his side! Perhaps I am angry with that type of woman because of my own experience. But, I am angry still the same.

"As for competing, I don't. If someone wants someone I have, it is up to him to decide. I refuse to play those games."

Elisa: "Competition often involves a man; but there are other ways to compete as well. You can compete over who has authority and favor over your children or someone else's. You can actually use your relationship with someone's children to hurt them."

Dorothy: "Yes, but I can't think of a better way to hurt another woman than to take her man. To me that is aggression of the worst kind. When you do that, you really make another woman question herself, her existence and sanity. Going after another woman's man is definitely competing or worse."

Sue: "I really don't get angry with other women. When I was younger, I spent much of my life angry with my mother for not fighting for my dad. They divorced and she spent much of her time in bed crying. I was angry also because she didn't fight for our happiness. She just became helpless. I think she should have competed with his mistress. She should have fought for us."

Wilma: "Not all mistresses mean to end up in a relationship with a married man. Sometimes things just happen. I am annoyed that these women are labeled manipulative. Sometimes you just wake up and find yourself in a competitive situation."

Madison: "How can you 'just wake up' and find yourself in a competitive situation that involves another woman's husband? Isn't that a choice? I don't understand why women say this. I find this very annoying."

Renée: "Life just happens. You do many things you never thought you'd do. Believe it or not, some of us haven't lived peachy lives. We've made mistakes. I personally find women who judge offensive."

Felicia: "I agree."

Mary: "It seems as if there is a lot of energy in this room today."

Allyson: "This is how life is. We have women who don't seem to understand the devastation that going with another woman's husband or boy friend causes. There are a lot of angry wives and girl friends out there. And in here too!"

Wilma: "I understand that, but we also have a lot of wives who take their husbands for granted."

Beth: "Who is responsible for an extra-marital affair?"

Elisa: "I think the married individual is responsible."

Bertha: "That's true, but what if the person was pushed away?"

Allyson: "I think the married person is responsible to seek some type of help, work harder, or end the marriage before they proceed into another relationship."

Mary: "Perhaps the guilty party is just using the outsider to take the pressure off."

Elisa: "I agree."

Sue: "Well, I would like to address how angry and disappointed I feel when I am abandoned by someone I thought was a friend."

Wilma: "I hope you are not talking about me. We work for the same employer."

Sue: "As a matter of fact, I am. I thought we had a friendship; but when I needed someone to talk to, you pulled away."

Wilma: "I don't consider us friends like close friends. It was nothing personal I have my own problems right now. You have other people to talk to."

Beth: "Tell me about the aggression in this room."

Mary: "There seems to be those who sympathize with extra-marital affairs and those who are against extra-marital affairs. Could it be that those who have perhaps had affairs are defending affairs and those who have been victimized by affairs are on the attack?"

Beth: "Attack?"

Wilma: "Yes, attack. That's how it feels."

Mary: "We want to be able to use this energy in a positive way."

Beth: "Absolutely. So here is what we are going to do. I will place two chairs in the middle of the floor, and I want each of you to take turns sitting in the speaker's chair.

"When in the speaker's chair, you can either speak to the wife of someone you have had an affair with or speak as the wife of someone who has had an affair. Or, you can address your own behavior in some type of triangle.

"The task for the onlookers is to understand the feelings of the speaker. It is the task of the speaker to take responsibility for her actions."

Silence fell upon the room as the women looked at each other. Felicia and Dorothy squirmed from side to side. Penny and Madison sat upright. Some of the women looked amazed, and others looked upward as if trying to retrieve information. Then Elsie ventured to take the speaker's chair and addressed the empty chair.

Elisa: "Friend, I felt betrayed by your decision to sleep with my husband. I was so deeply affected that I would not allow myself to be placed in that situation again.

"I became a woman on a mission to inflict pain. My decision to close myself off from females resulted in intimacy issues with my so called girl friends. When I felt females getting too close or spending too much time with me, I retreated.

"Since then, I have experienced a significant emotional event which led to positive transformation in my hapless life. I made a conscious choice to no longer be a victim to your irresponsible choices. I now choose to no longer hurt other women. I choose to release myself from the friendship prison I have built."

Dorothy: [With tears in her eyes, Dorothy began to speak.] "Wife, I apologize for sleeping with your husband. I apologize for allowing him to bounce between your sheets and mine. I apologize to your children and mine for decreasing the quality of their lives. I apologize to our daughters for teaching them, through my behavior, that they are not worth a full-time father and a full-time lover.

"I apologize to your sons because they have been taught to model after their father. I apologize to the women I don't know who will be affected by your husband's behavior. I apologize for thinking so little of myself."

Melanie: "I apologize to my daughters for not always having the strength to say no to men. I apologize for going to the opposite extreme and wanting them to have a step-father so badly that I was sometimes desperate. In my desperation, I was really trying to fulfill my own needs."

Bertha: "I apologize to my children for picking two husbands who were unavailable much of the time. I will stay in my current marriage and learn more about myself – why I pick cheaters."

Renée: "I would like to apologize to all the women whose husbands I have been with. I have lived most of my life doing whatever felt good at the time. Life has been one big party, and I have not lived responsibly. I can no longer defend my actions; I was wrong."

Allyson: "I would like to learn to listen to my fiancée. I want to create a safe place for him to be human and imperfect. I want to be creative and sensuous. I want to continue to look good, smell good, and make time for us. I don't want life to just happen. I don't want to take him for granted. I don't want to ever stop growing and encouraging him to grow. I want to always make time for him only, even when the children come."

Wilma: "Wife, you did not tell him how handsome he looked. You were always running off with your friends and trying to get a promotion to management. At first, I tried to help you out by sending him home. But you were never there. I told him to be patient and that you'd come around. I told him about his faults and excused yours.

"I saw a man filled with tension. He cried on my shoulder. At first, I felt nothing when I would put my arms around him. I sent him home even when I was filled with sexual tension. I became angry with you. I hated you for not wanting your blessings.

"I begged God every night for someone like him and frankly, I got tired of begging. It wasn't planned. It just happened. Both our hearts ached. We both had needs. Now both our futures are undecided. Our children will suffer. I apologize to our unborn children. I apologize to you."

The air in the room was thick with tension and Mary's eyes met mine. Could this be an accident? Our eye contact was interrupted by Sue's shoulders which suddenly began to jerk up and down as she stood to take the speaker's seat.

Sue: "I don't sleep. I have lost weight. How could you? I thought better of you. You were supposed to be my friend. I found your card in his pants pocket; and I dismissed it, giving credit to you. How could I be such a fool? He was mine.

"We took vows before God. You had no right to use him. Were you trying to destroy me? Was your conquest for sport? How dare you?

"My Lord! I am pregnant. How selfishly heartless? You betrayed and abandoned me. You ripped my heart out and pissed on it."

When Sue returned to her seat, I passed her a tissue.

Elisa was horrified as tears swelled in her eyes. She identified with this situation and was surprised that the pain of yesteryears was still there. She knew just how Sue felt. She had been there countless times. She could not escape the pain of her past which had once again become a part of her present reality.

Elisa: "It has been twenty-five years since my discovery that my best friend was sleeping with my husband. Sue, I understand your pain. I wish I could tell you that it will get better, but I can't. I *can* say that you can learn to live with the pain. Perhaps as a result of this group experience we will learn to deal with our betrayals better."

Felicia sensed what was happening and decided to rescue Wilma by reflecting on her own past.

Felicia: "In the past, I have not considered what you may be going through as a result of my actions. After your husband died, I thought of only my own grief.

"I now realize that I stole so much precious time from you. I know that you must have many unanswered questions. I see that in your face when I see you in the office. I realize that as a result of growing up angry, I have pimped men; just the way men pimp women. But, I really did love him. He was different."

(Pause)

"I take responsibility for all the hurt and pain I have caused."

Madison: "This is hard for me because I have developed such a thick protective skin and I rarely allow people to see who I am. I mask the pain by being a sweet and efficient first lady. I hurt when I see my husband go bonkers over slim, educated, and together women. It's not easy making sure everything is under control in our church, and I make sure I am indispensable. I know more about the business than he does. So, although he goes out and charms people, I make sure he cannot survive without me.

"Sometimes I really wish I had completed school so that my life could be lived for me instead of for the church or through my husband. I think I have been angry for a long time: angry that I didn't finish school, angry that my sisters are attorneys, angry that they are so fashionable, angry that my home does not compare with theirs.

"After I clothe our kids, I am lucky if I end up with a grossly over-priced tent from out of the fat lady's store. I realize that I must release what I have no control over and focus on my individual happiness. Although it appears that I am succeeding, in truth I am failing miserably."

Penny: "This is difficult for me, too. I have spent my life staying on top of situations. I learned that from watching my mother. The only thing that I remember being angry about is her doting over my siblings so much. My brother was '*boy-dream-do-no-evil.*' My sister was '*sister-sick.*' Unlike me, they both got plenty of attention. If I got attention at all, it was for efficiency.

"Now I really don't allow another woman to hurt me because I am on top of things. The only thing that I can think of that may anger me is when someone gets in my way or when they don't cooperate."

Jasmine: "I am angered by injustice, pain and deception. I think there is far too much of it in the world. I feel responsible to try and make injustices just, and ease pain, and make truth clear in my own little corner."

Now that everyone had had an opportunity to have their say, the chair was empty. I continued the session by having the group focus on what had transpired.

Beth: "Tell me about the energy in the room tonight."

Jasmine: "I think the room is filled with released tension, deep pains, and problems."

Beth: "What type of problems?"

Allyson: "We have expressed regret, betrayal, anger, envy, and other feelings that we may or may not have been handling well up to now."

Mary: "Yes, and I think some of these feeling involve the men in our lives; some involve our families of origin; and some just involve our own feelings. One of the things I heard was much attention given to extra-marital affairs."

Dorothy: "I heard that also. Speaking as a woman who has engaged in extra-marital activity, I am really sorry. Seducing men is an easy game. And, then you have your fun. Which, might I add, usually lasts for a short while. But, after it's over you have really caused lots of pain. The wife or girl friend is in pain. You are in pain. The children are in pain. You may not believe this; but if he develops feelings for you, even he is in pain. And, you really didn't want the man, usually. I loved the idea of winning."

Sue: "What do you mean seducing men is easy?"

Dorothy: "Honey, that's the fun part. I know there are wives in here, and I am one also. At least now I am. You just don't understand."

Jasmine: "Are you saying that there are women just waiting for us to mess up at home?"

Dorothy: "Exactly! And, there are women who see messing your marriage up as a challenge. And, then there's the stuff that just happens because the husband is not satisfied."

Renée: "I have met many married men who are simply on the prowl for women. They tell women how easy and how good their wives have it. They say stuff like: she gets to keep all of her check and yet she can't pay the bills on time. I provide everything.

"Some women, who are naive, may think that the wife is ungrateful. But, the experienced woman listens and knows where the relationship is going. She just makes sure she gets something other than sex from it. Dorothy you are absolutely right. Seductions are a breeze."

Madison was shocked but decided to take advantage of the opportunity in order to protect her marriage.

Madison: "I'd like to learn about the different ways to seduce men."

Dorothy: "Well, there is the *emotional seduction*. You test them with 'Do you understand that I am on your side?' When they believe you understand them, then you keep implying that the wife doesn't understand."

Wilma fidgeted uncomfortably.

"Then there is the *financial seduction*. You test them by demonstrating a need to be rescued by such an affluent man. When he helps you, you know your foot is in the door because men tend to stick with their investments. And women, for some men, are thought of as investments."

Renée nodded in agreement.

"Then there is the traditional *damsel in distress* seduction. These women profess 'poor helpless, dumb me; I need a man to help me do whatever.' This one is used a lot in mainstream America."

Renée: "Don't forget the seduction of *secret keeping*."

Dorothy: "Oh, yes, the seduction of *secret keeping*. You encourage secrets between their husband and you. When he keeps those secrets from his wife; you solidify your position. Soon the sex will be secretive, also."

Renée: "Then it's the *sexual seduction*. You know, 'Do you like what you see? Would you like a bite of my apple?'

Elisa: "I imagine you can also seduce men by your *brilliance*. Although this is what men usually do to us."

Dorothy: "I've seen this happen, too. Although I really can't say that I am smooth enough or smart enough to do that one. This one is for brainiacs. It's really easy for a smart woman to connect to a man who values brilliance."

Elisa: "Oh yeah, and what about *parental seductions*. Sometime people go after your kids. They side with the kids and speak against the parents. Friends, grandmothers, aunts and other family members do this. There are a whole lot of these power plays in families, and mine has been no exception."

Jasmine: "Speaking of power plays! *Power* is a means of seducing. People want to side with power. There are some women who understand and know how to use power. But, I don't think their seduction is sexual. It's mental."

Bertha: "Yeah, but do they get the same high as a sexual high?"

Dorothy: "Girl, for some folk a power seduction trumps a sexual seduction any day of the week."

Renée laughed.

Renée: "Yeah, and the more seductions you have going at a time; the better the sex."

Beth: "We have discussed many feelings and concerns today. These concerns dealt with our anger, betrayals, emotions, and dilemmas. Remember, what we discuss in here is confidential and stays in here. Please know that it is not our intention to cause anyone harm. In fact, if you feel that you have been harmed or that you have concerns about continuing in this group, please see Mary or me tonight. If you find that you have concerns after we leave, please call us."

Mary: "We'll continue next week at the same time and be prepared to take a look at our families."

Chapter 15 – Processing Session Two

As I reviewed the session with Mary, I began with an utterance that I had been suppressing since the group was in session, "Oh my goodness, please tell me that this did not just happen!"

"I wish I could."

"How did it happen?"

Equally blown away, Mary reviewed how we found ourselves at this place, "Well, let's see…. Wilma learned of the group through Madison, her new pastor's wife. Remember, we placed an ad in Madison's church bulletin. She was a member of the first focus group. Obviously, she responded."

True, but I was still perplexed, "Come on now. There was no way we could anticipate Wilma's relationship with Sue's husband. But we don't know how Sue learned of the group. Perhaps it was through our other advertisements.

"Obviously she responded. There was no way we could anticipate Wilma joining this church and collaborating with Madison. Sue, on the other hand, probably learned of the group through a friend of mine, Estelle Devereaux. Estelle has a prayer ministry. Then we conducted separate interviews for the sake of time. But, we should have interviewed them together. Talk about Murphy's Law!"

"I talked with one of Estelle's prayer partners before we decided to have a group," said Mary, but I don't think it was Sue. I believe her name was Cynthia."

"Did she mention having spoken with me during the interview?"

"No."

"Do you think this was intentional?" I inquired.

"Of course not."

At this point, I could not see any sign of intent. They had no way of knowing about the other's decision unless it was through Preston or someone at work.

"I am exhausted," Mary exclaimed, reminding me that we had put in a hard day's work of preparing for the session and conducting it.

"I know. Keeping up with everyone's emotional status is terribly exhausting."

"Okay, now what?" Mary asked.

"We consult with Dr. Lipscomb."

"Good choice. Other than this colossal turn of events, the session went well."

"I agree."

Chapter 16 – Consultations

Dr. Lipscomb agreed that we had witnessed a rare and unfortunate turn of events, "I really don't think this was planned by anyone. However, I must say that in my sixteen years of supervising groups, this has never happened before.

"If you ask Wilma to discontinue, you risk appearing as if you have judged her openly. By doing so, you damage the process. If you ask Sue to discontinue, you risk the same. Now, from what you have told me, the group appears to be dividing into three categories: sympathizers with extramarital affairs, those against extramarital affairs, and the neutrals. This should really make your storming very interesting.

"However, ultimately it is your responsibility to make sure these ladies feel safe. When it appears obvious to everyone what is happening, make it very clear that this group is not a battle ground for their personal fights.

"Until then, you cannot use information gained outside the group for your work with the group. Nor can you discuss intent or the sequence of events leading up to the women joining the group with anyone outside the group. Futher, do not allow either of these women to put you in a situation that entices you to discuss the other apart from the group.

"Okay you are in week what?"

"Three," I answered.

"How many weeks is your group scheduled to run?"

"Ten."

"Okay, I really need profiles on these women."

"We'll get right on it. But, we need a little more time for the performance stage to kick-in."

"They should be on my desk immediately after group six. You should be performing by then. Is there anything else I can help you with Mary?"

"No. Thank you Dr. Lipscomb. I left my bag in the lounge, so if I am finished I will excuse myself."

"Thank you, Mary. Beth?"

"Not at this time. Thank you very much," I responded.

"Beth."

"Yes."

"Where are you going with all this?"

"Well, I hope to use information from the focus group and information from the encounter group to develop a survey and test my hypothesis on a larger scale.

"Until now, I have had the hardest time finding literature that called relational aggression abuse. But, I have found literature that suggests if men and women execute the same hostile behavior toward women; the women's behavior would be called relational aggression and the men's behavior would be called abuse [Evans, 1994]. Perhaps this is a rock that needs to be turned over and investigated"

"This is my last semester of course work. I am taking my comprehensives in June. I plan to finish my pilot study and finish my proposal this summer. Of course, none of the women in the focus group or encounter group can participate in the pilot study."

Dr. Lipscomb then inquired, "Have you selected a chair?"

"I was hoping to ask you," I responded, hopefully.

"Would this theory be substantiated by interviews or data?"

"Data, of course. We all know in our spirits that this thing exists."

"But, has it been proven with numbers?"

"No," I answered.

"Proceed," said Dr. Lipscomb.

"Well, I would like to expand upon my list of behaviors women consider abuse. Then I would like to give it some type of reliability by asking expert judges to determine just what behaviors they consider abuse. When this is done, I would have established inter rater agreement."

"Who are your expert judges?"

"They haven't been selected yet, but I was thinking of using psychotherapists already practicing, mental health professors, that type of professional.

"Then I would like to develop a survey using these agreed-upon abuses and administer it to women of different ages, races, regions, incomes, and educational levels, you know, a general administration. Of course, I would have some superfluous information on the survey."

"Yes. Continue."

"I will do this by asking three simple questions. Question one: What behaviors do women consider abuse? Question two: To what extent are these perceptions of abuse/mistreatment related to gender profile? Question three: To what extent are the personal experiences as victims or perpetrators of abuse related to age, race, and education?

"I am in the process of writing a major research paper in your Women's Studies class which has propelled me far into my literature review."

"Brilliant! What are your hypotheses?"

"I would look at age, race and educational levels. I would also look at gender profiles and if the women perceive they have been abused or have abused other women."

"Now, you said you were thinking of asking me to be your chair."

"Yes, I would very much like for you to be the chairwoman of my doctoral dissertation."

"I accept your invitation." We both smiled broad, warm smiles as we wrapped up our time together.

Gaining a chair made the drive home very short. I could not wait to tell Robert and the boys the good news. Upon reaching home, I found dinner was already prepared. German potato salad minus the bacon, mixed green salad, Big Franks, and home-made hot dog buns were ready for consumption.

Robert could manage the Big Franks, but the German potato salad and home-made buns were no doubt the work of Mrs. Blumfeld. Who by the way was seated in the nook?

'Honey, I invited Mrs. Blumfeld to eat dinner with us this evening."

"Sure, please join us, Mrs. Blumfeld.

"Amen" was the last word of grace. *Now, I could tell them.*

Placing a frank onto his bun, Robert broke some news, "Honey, Estelle is in the hospital."

"What? When? Why?"

Aaron and Jason lowered their heads.

"She seems to have taken a turn for the worse."

"She did not want you to know because she doesn't want you to stop your research," chimed Mrs. Blumfeld.

"My God, I have been so consumed with me and school that I haven't even bothered to call her and check on her."

"I understand and so does she. I have been checking on her for you. Her son is coming to get her this weekend to take her back to his hometown to see an herbalist."

"Isn't her son a doctor? Is it that bad? Has traditional medicine given up? I am sorry. I have neglected all of you."

"Nonsense child, you haven't neglected anyone; we have supported you. Estelle believes you are doing important work, and so do we. She asked me months ago to watch over you and I intend to do just that. She expects for us to have a lovely supper, and she is expecting your call later."

* * *

"Hello, Estelle. This is Beth."

"Hi, Beth. How is school coming?"

"Never you mind about school. How are you?"

"Listen, Beth. I will so mind about school. Baby, your research is your purpose. When I met you, I thought the world of you and I took you for my daughter. I knew there was something we shared in common. I knew that you have been harassed and abused by females all of your life. Darling, birds of a feather recognize their own.

"But, listen to me and listen to me carefully. I am more afraid of those women than I am the cancer within my body. I rest assured in the promise that your research will make a difference. It will bring emotional healing to women who don't understand the forces of darkness. The pain we inflict leaves deep traumatic scars that seemingly never go away.

"But you went down front! You said you were healed!

"Beth, I have faith. Besides, I have learned that not all healing is physical. Spiritual healing is more important than physical healing. Now I must thank you."

"For what? Neglecting you?"

"Child you did not neglect me. You helped me. I did not have a relationship with my daughter. I did not know how blessed I could be with a mother-daughter relationship. Remember, my mother died when I was fifteen years old. I did not know how to be a good mother and how to protect my family. I lost my husband and my daughter.

"But God is faithful. He knew the pains of my heart. I talked to Him for years; and at last, I met you. Thank you for not turning your back on me that day in your kitchen. I needed you and I sensed you were safe.

"I was a part of the birthday parties for the kids, dinners after church, your family worships. You brought lesson studies to me when I could not get out to church. You have not neglected me. And, Mrs. Blumfeld has been bringing all the food over for you since you have been in school."

"Oh, my goodness! Mrs. Blumfeld!!!"

"I have not been neglected," she continued. I have been loved in the way that I needed loving the most. God used you and your family's arms to reach out and hold me when I needed holding the most. Beth, He is a gooood God. Now tell me, where you are in your process."

"Well, I am taking my last two classes and since these classes don't require finals; I have begun to study for my comprehensive exams this coming June. I am also doing the foundation work for my dissertation. The proposal should be ready later this summer. My educational leave has been granted, so I will not return to work this fall and I will be able to analyze my surveys and write full time."

"Praise God, Beth! You must finish the book. Finish this for your mother and for the women who have been damaged by other women; finish so women can receive healing and experience change. Finish this for me."

Chapter 17 – Performance Profiles

The faculty offices were abandoned the next evening. No doubt, most of the professors were either teaching or had gone home for the day. Dr. Lipscomb's mailbox wasn't full, so I was able to neatly place the large envelope containing the profiles inside the box. Thinking, "Well, wait," I retrieved the envelope and browsed my cover letter and report one last time.

Dear Dr. Lipscomb,

Here are the requested performance profiles of the women in the focus group. I have divided them into four groups: "1) women who perceive they have been abused by other women, 2) women who perceive they have abused other women, 3) women who perceive they have neither abused nor been abused by other women, and 4) women who perceive that they have both abused other women and been abused by other women.

I have changed their names to protect confidentiality.

Category 1: Women Who Perceive They Have Been Abused By Other Women

#1 (Melanie)

#1 presents as a 29-year-old single female who is the head of the household. She is the oldest child of three siblings, dropped out of traditional high school after a pregnancy, and graduated from a vocational high school after studying cosmetology.

Presenting issues include low ego strength, poor judgment, and an inability to discern intent in others.

Goals established by the therapeutic team are as follows: 1) to increase ego strength and 2) to learn to set boundaries.

#1's definitions of abuse lack structure as she sees herself a victim in various circumstances. Her feelings of being abused and her inability to define abuse create disequilibrium. Although she appears to draw strength from the women in the group, she seeks approval. Her ability to generalize new skills from the therapeutic setting to her functional life is at this time questionable.

Professional opinions are that #1 is stronger than she believes and the positive coaching beyond the encounter experience is questioned.

Diagnostic Impression: Dependent Personality Disorder characterized by difficulty making everyday decisions; need for others to assume responsibility for most major areas in her life; has difficulty expressing disagreement with others because of fear of loss of support or approval; goes to excessive lengths to obtain nurturance and support from others and urgently seeks replacement relationships at the outset of a relationship.

Defense mechanism: Compliance and identification.

#2 (Bertha)

#2 presents as a 39-year-old former minister's wife who is presently married to a police officer. She exhibits a calm affect and has worked through much of her psychoanalytic work independently. She expresses that she has married her unavailable father twice in her life and is presently concerned that her husband maintain emotional availability for her children.

Her effort to secure emotional availability for her children is hampered by her husband's preference to work the midnight shift and sleep late in the day. She reports knowing of her father's affairs and her first husband's affairs with women in his church. She suspects her present husband of having had at least two affairs during their marriage.

#2's definition of abuse includes emotional unavailability, failure to support, and withdrawal of affection. She postulates that "women can be each other's worst enemies or dearest treasures." She maintains good relations with her mother, sister, and two best friends.

#2's therapeutic goals are as follows: 1) learn to express emotional needs and 2) understand why she has accepted disloyalty in her husbands.

Diagnostic Impression: Relational problem.

#3 (Sue)

#3 presents as a 39 year-old married woman experiencing marital tension which has resulted in a triangulated affair on the part of her husband and a co-worker who is also a member of the encounter group. She is the only child to her parents.

Although #3 shares a group experience with her husband's former mistress, she and the mistress are productively working on civility. Her definition of abuse includes betrayal, extramarital affairs, and breach of marital sacredness. Therapeutic goals are as followed: "1) taking responsibility for the break down in her marital relationship, 2) using anger toward the other woman in a productive way, and 3) making wise decisions regarding her and her husband's unborn children.

Diagnostic Impression: Adjustment Disorder with Depression.

Category 2: Women Who Perceive They Have Abused Other Women

#4 (Madison)

#4 is a 49-year-old woman who is experiencing existential anxiety regarding her accomplishments in life. She reflects much on her past choices and has difficulty staying in the here-and-now as far as her presence in the group is concerned.

#4 expresses she has demonstrated a passive aggressive personality and wishes to become more assertive and expressive. She believes she was "led" to the encounter group and projects that her experience in the group will have a positive and unique impact on her ministry.

Although there is no formal diagnosis, #4 has experienced disequilibrium in what Erik Erikson refers to as Identity vs. Identity Confusion. She failed to develop the autonomy to have a well established progression through the next stage, Intimacy vs. Isolation.

During her period of Intimacy vs. Isolation, namely in young adulthood, #4 became consumed with the identity of her newly wedded husband and his participation in a popular group. As her husband and his group became increasingly popular, she became less secure, thus developing intimacy issues.

As a result of early success and identification in the limelight, she continued to seek adoration from the general population. She enjoys the fame, but still finds trusting people difficult. She admittedly verbalizes and is aware of her intimacy and trust issues and wishes to work to correct these issues. After working on her issues, she hopes to help younger women understand the impact of healthy relationships with the men in their lives and with other women.

Goals established by the therapeutic team are as follows: 1) to understand and use her gifts positively, 2) to clearly define her identity, 3) to take responsibility for her life choices, and 4) to determine what is purposeful living.

Her definition of women abusing other women includes keeping women at a distance, keeping individuals on the outside of inner circles, manipulating weak women, withdrawing affection in order to control women, and not support the efforts of potentially powerful women. #4 excuses her behavior stating that she has "simply done what she was taught to do."

Diagnostic Impression: Relational problem; Phase of life problems. Defense mechanism: Altruism.

#5 (Wilma)

#5 is a 27 year-old single woman who is on the outset of an extramarital affair with her co-workers husband. Her co-worker, #3, is also a member of the encounter group. #5, expressed desires that her unborn child have a relationship with its father and its unborn sibling, which is also the unborn child of #3. #5 has accepted responsibility for her actions and has reports that she has "turned over a new lease in life." This "new lease" includes her recent membership in a church community.

The goal established by the therapeutic team is as follows: "to increase self-awareness.

Her definition of women abusing other women includes intent to hurt another person.

Diagnostic Impression: Relational problem.

#6 (Renée)

#6 is a 36-year-old single woman who lives with her mother and daughter.

She has recently become a displaced automobile worker and is experiencing some ambivalence regarding the meaning of her life, her behavior, and her choices. Her presentation is authentic as she endeavors to gain maximum benefit from her therapeutic setting.

Goals established by the therapeutic team are as follows: 1) to examine the benefits available as a result of career displacement and 2) to redefine the self.

Her definition of women abusing other women includes sleeping with another woman's husband and violating a space in a marriage that is rightfully set for a wife.

Diagnostic Impression: Relational problems and problems with unemployment.

#7 (Dorothy)

#7 is a 56-year-old who, after six months of dating, married an incarcerated man. Psychoanalytic work revealed a turbulent relationship in her family of origin between her mother and father and between her father and siblings.

According to #7, father was charismatic in public and abusive in the privacy of their home. Attempts to seek control over the type of helplessness displayed by her mother and maintain identification with father have resulted in choosing unavailable men. Choosing unavailable men allowed her to maintain autonomy while being intimately connected with an individual of the opposite sex.

Goals established by the therapeutic team are as follows: 1) to understand the effects of her family of origin on her present behavior, 2) to increase ego strength, and 3) to remain grounded in the presence of emotional turbulence.

Her definition of women abusing other women includes sleeping with another woman's husband, betrayal, verbalizing hurtful messages, yelling, and refusing to acknowledge a woman's presence.

Diagnostic Impression: Relational problem. Defense mechanism: Humor, avoidance.

Category 3: Women Who Perceive They Have Neither Abused Nor Been Abused By Other Women

#8 (Allyson)

#8 presents as a 39-year-old single woman who is a student at the University. She is completing a graduate degree in Social Work and is a leader in the community. She is the only daughter and is the youngest child with four male siblings. According to #8, her parents are nurturing and are supportive of each sibling. As a result of their positive home life, each sibling has chosen careers in the human service arena.

#8 is proactive and has a positive outlook on life. She maintains good relations with her parents, siblings, fellow students, and church members. #8's definition of abuse includes: betrayal, gossip, manipulation, and controlling others to the point that it interferes with their growth.

Therapeutic goals are as follows: 1) to experience group dynamics and 2) expansion of her breadth of knowledge.

Her definition of women abusing other women includes any unreasonable measure intended to bring pain, especially in a subordinate/insubordinate relationship.

Diagnostic Impression: No Diagnosis. Defense mechanism: Altruism.

#9 (Jasmine)

#8 is a calm 42-year-old who lives in a community thirty miles east of the University. She is insightful and offers sound advice to other members of the group. #8 has emerged as the group leader. Her spirituality is demonstrated in the advice she gives. She reports that she spends much of her discretionary time working on social events and for social causes.

Her definition of abuse includes any harmful treatment of a person which is contrary to their intended purpose.

Diagnostic Impression: No diagnosis. Defense mechanism: Altruism.

Category 4: Women Who Perceive That They Have Both Abused Other Women and Been Abused by Other Women

#10 (Felicia)

#10 is a 56-year-old divorcee who presents as quiet and unadorned. She has actively participated in group discussions and self-examination. #10 has come to the understanding of why she exploits men and has contributed her behavior as a counter-reaction to behavior modeled by her mother. #10's perception was that her mother was physically and financially exploited by men. She claims she was damaged as a result.

Goals established by the therapeutic team are as follows: 1) to understand the effects of her family of origin on her present behavior, and 2) to understand how her behavior affects her children's behavior.

Her definition of abuse involves yelling, demeaning, and belittling, breaking down another woman's will, refusing to acknowledge another woman's presence, and hurting another woman by sleeping with her husband.

Diagnostic Impression: Relational problem. Defense mechanism: Deception.

#11 (Elisa)

#11 is a 56-year-old twice divorced woman whose first marriage ended as a result of domestic violence and whose second marriage ended as a result of incompatibility.

Family history involves a close relationship with her grandma Hazel during her childhood and adolescence. During childhood and adolescence, #11 also experienced a tumultuous relationship with her mother, Betty, and spent much of her time with her grandma Hazel.

According to #11, she and her daughter, Ivory, also experienced a tumultuous relationship during Ivory's childhood and adolescent years. During Ivory's childhood and adolescence, she shared an amicably close relationship with her maternal grandmother, Betty, in much the same way #11 had a relationship with her maternal grandmother, Hazel. Both #11 and her mother, Betty, bore one son and one daughter and favored their sons over their daughters."

As a result of intimacy issues in #11's family and the reinforcement of these issues on more than one occasion in adult life, Elisa appears to have a difficult time sustaining intimacy with females for long periods of time and finds a need for space when relationships become "too" close.

As a result of physical abuse perpetrated by her first husband, #11 is also easily disenfranchised with relationships with men in that when they pursue her she is flattered; however panics when the man pursues intimacy and commitment. She is success driven, works long hours, and often uses competence as a defense mechanism. Clinical goals are: 1) assess for co-existing psychological disorders, 2) refer for pharmacological consultation, and 3) retard re-experiencing specific traumas.

Her definition of abuse involves physical and emotional scarring, betrayal, and back-stabbing.

Diagnostic Impression: Post Traumatic Stress Disorder. Defense mechanism: Avoidance, competence.

#12 (Penny)

Penny is a school administrator who is highly active in her church community. Thus far she has functioned in the role of the "help-rejecting complainer" and has doubts that a woman can abuse another woman. Her presence creates a balance in the therapeutic setting because her doubts elicit critical thinking in other participants. Although her analytic skills are superior, they may be detrimental in that she uses intellectualism as a defense mechanism.

#12 appears to be in denial of some of her actions, in that she has clearly described instances where she has caused injury to others. She often justifies her actions and presents an innocent demeanor. Yet, when under grueling inquisition by other group members, she initially becomes irritated, but regroups and calmly presents herself as a victim and others as perpetrators.

She maintains that easy-going women need guidance, not acknowledging someone's presence is often not intentional, giving unsolicited opinions is needed, and keeping women at a distance and avoiding them because of their friends are acceptable behaviors.

#12 also maintains that gossip is normal, betrayal is a part of life and that women in the group are making much too much over natural occurrences. She states any good "administrator must protect their programs." When asked to clarify these and other statements, she is vague.

Goals established by the therapeutic team are: 1) to understand the effects of her family of origin on her present behavior and 2) to empathize with the women in the group.

Defense mechanism: Projection. She states that people do not like her when she does not like others.

Diagnostic Impression: Narcissistic personality traits. Passive Aggressive Personality. Relational problem.

Summary

Although diagnostic impressions are included in the above profiles, adequate assessment appears to be problematic when referencing the Diagnostic and Statistical Manual. The diagnosis of Relational Problems appears to be a common thread among the participants. Although relational difficulties are present, many of the women suffer from a mild form of Post Traumatic Stress Disorder.

In this milder form of Post Traumatic Stress Disorder, "treatment from other females" is often named as the identifiable stressor. This stressor is reportedly experienced through relationships with other women, whether inclusive or exclusive of the participant's nuclear family.

In some more pronounced cases, such as the case with #11, it appears that the client experiences multiple incidences of stressful situations regarding women. In response to these stressors, #11 developed behaviors which include estrangement from women, distrust of women, panic in social situations with women, and panic when in intimate relationships with both females and males. #11 also developed defense mechanisms, including avoidance and inflicting pain before it is inflicted.

Although #11's case is more pronounced, the same distrust and estrangement is presented by the majority of women in the group. Note that relationship issues began with #11 before she entered into a relationship with her abusive/violent husband. Similar issues were noted in #3 and #7.

Participants #1, #4, #5, #6, and #10 all reported relational issues early in life. Although not expected, many of these relationship problems can be traced to modeling of the participants' mothers. As such, we are requesting two additional weeks of therapeutic intervention with this group.

Submitted by: Beth Johnson

Chapter 18 – Rage

Lightning flashed and thunder rolled … but not loudly enough to override the expletives screamed by Warmouth: "You imbeciles! How could you not report this group?????"

One soldier lifted his head, explaining, "There is prayer coverage inside the group."

Okus, the tactical specialist, shivered and added, "We didn't know until our inside woman came home complaining of their progress to the women in her court. She is becoming affected by the progress of the others, and now our enemy is wrestling with her day and night. We may lose her, Sir.

"Find the inside problem and report to me tomorrow. You will fix this, or you will all be demoted to imps," threatened Warmouth.

The small company of demons trembled. They knew Warmouth meant exactly what he said. Before they could look at one another, Warmouth leaped into the dark night sky and moved on to another sinister setting.

"Okay," said Bentler, "Who are the participants in the group?"

"Let's see," responded Okus. "We have Mary Mathews and Beth Johnson as leaders. The participants are Felicia Terrell, Elisa Nixon, Penny King, Melanie Robinson, Dorothy Scott, Madison Gathers, Wilma Bryant, Bertha Harvey, Sue Gaston, Renée Mason, Allyson Akins, and Jasmine Rivers."

"Great! Quickly summon the soldiers assigned to them and let's get busy," ordered Okus.

Eleven soldiers were there within 15 minutes. Puzzled, Bentler asked, "Where is the twelfth soldier?"

With regret Okus responded, "Sir, we could only find eleven." Bentler fell on the floor and fumed as his body and the earth below him trembled. Recovering, he stated, "Do you idiots mean to tell me that you let a soldier from the other side penetrate the group? We are doomed."

In an attempt at damage control, Okus responded, " Let's divide this group so that we can plan our strategies."

Recovering, Bentler commanded, "Okay, let's determine who the Christians are. Then, let's work on this group.

"First, we will consider the Christians who do not pray. Let's just throw some detours their way. Second, we will focus on the occasional pray-ers; they should be easy. We will double their detail.

"Third, we will focus on the Christians who pray daily. Interrupt their prayer schedules. Make them fall asleep while praying. Have them remember things they must do that day. Better yet, have them remember things they have forgotten to do. Provide them with close substitutes to answered prayer so they will think they will no longer have a need to pray.

"After we attack these two groups, we will go for the grand slam – the Christians who read the Bible and self-examine daily. I want to exploit the weaknesses in their characters, their family curses, their idiosyncrasies, and their genetic predispositions."

After careful pondering, Okus responded, "Sir, this means we will focus on Wilma Bryant, Madison Gathers, Mary Mathews, and Beth Johnson. Wilma has recently gone over to the other side. She is pregnant by another member's husband. If we attack her now, we can cause inner turmoil within the group and get her back.

"Perhaps we can work with Sue so that she won't allow her husband to have any contact with the baby. Surely, we can send our Anger detail into the room through Wilma.

"Madison Gathers prays daily and has begun to negatively [for us] change the traditional ideas within her church. This can't be tolerated.

Mary Mathews has a history of breast cancer and, although not cancerous yet, has two tumors in her breast. Beth Johnson's husband has a degenerative disease in his DNA. By the way, I will get a soldier from our Insecurity Unit in that room through Penny King. We've used her many times in the past."

Great, Okus, this is a start. We will place an order so that when our Commander-in-Chief comes before the Holy One, he will requisition our most grievous trials. Stay on top of this and let me know as soon as we get an answer.

* * *

Warmouth related the discouraging set of parameters sent from the Evil One to the sinister brood waiting to implement their devilish attack on the focus group. To their disappointment, they learned that their carefully hatched plans could not go forth.

"What, we cannot touch one hair on their heads??!!! This cannot be!

"Well, we will attack where we can! This is not over! We will win this battle! I will not become an imp!" fumed Okus.

"We may not be able to touch Wilma; but, Preston is definitely ours. Boost his ego and cause him to pit Wilma and his wife, Sue, against one another. Have Preston tell Sue just what he liked about Wilma. Once those words are out, they will rumble around in Sue's pretty little head. We will use them to torment her. Then we will hit Sue with a triple cocktail: Insecurity, Jealously, and Control. She will go after Wilma eventually.

"Act upon Wilma's family history, and exacerbate her shame. Wilma has unresolved feelings about being abandoned by her father. She won't be able to separate the shame she feels from being a child born out of wedlock from the shame she is experiencing from having a child out of wedlock. Don't we have a clique of women in Wilma's new church that can help us with this detail? If we can get her shame inflamed, she will accept Anger as a defense mechanism. We may not be able to touch her physically; but, we will trample on her emotions."

"Madison and her husband are rather ambitious. We need a scandal to divert Madison's attention. Look for a young attractive woman to flirt with her husband, the pastor. If he shows interest, lure him in by having them share secrets.

"But, don't stop there. Lay several snares for him. We need a financial trap. Check out the integrity of the church treasurer. Try to get him to purchase a few nice trinkets for Madison. Then have them overextend themselves financially. Tempt him to go for another salary increase without board approval. Better yet, help him mesmerize his financial committee.

"Keep Madison off-center so she will give up her ridiculous notion of changing the subculture of women. Over the centuries, we have worked diligently to maintain treachery in this subculture. We cannot lose ground now."

Pausing to collect his thoughts, Okus prepared to continue, "Yes, where was I? I want Mary Mathews to experience a tremendous amount of stress as she writes and defends her dissertation. Have her committee tear up her writing and ignore the methods which they have already instructed. We can't touch her body, but we can cause enough stress so that her tumors should calcify and become cancerous. Attack her children. Make them sick.

"Beth Johnson's husband has degenerative genes in chromosomes 1, 14, and 21. Make them mutate even faster! Check out his diet. Make him want all the wrong foods. Make him crave sugar and reject vegetables. Use him to weaken her faith and distract her. Have Gossip place blame upon the tongues of the women in her church. Make the women tell him that his illness is God's wrath against him for marrying her. Better yet, accuse her of making him sick. Then turn his anger against her. Leave no stone unturned. She is our main target. Destroy her at all costs."

* * *

It was two o'clock in the morning and all was well in the Park. Robert and I were lying on our backs asleep when Robert's chest began to heave with arrhythmic breathing. Unaware that he was clutching his chest, Robert gave a guttural yell that started low in intensity and quickly escalated. Robert's stiff body quickly turned to his left side and fell from the mattress against the writing desk beside the bed, then to the floor below.

Screaming, I ran around the bed and witnessed his jerking on the floor next to the bed.

"My God! Robert!" she exclaimed. Aaron! Help!"

Recognizing what was happening; I cleared the furniture around Robert's head, rolled him over onto his side, and glanced at the clock near his head.

Aaron and Jason ran into the bedroom. "What? What?" asked Aaron.

"Aaron, call 911 and tell them to send an ambulance, Robert is having a seizure.

"Jason, run across the street and get Dr. Carver."

Without a word, Jason turned and ran into the night air. "Now, Aaron, look how I am protecting his head and keeping him on his side. Do exactly what I am doing while I get dressed."

"Okay, I will take over, Mom."

"Now, clear all the furniture out of the way between this room and the front door."

The seizure began to dissipate. At 2:15, Robert was able to moan. Around 2:25, I noticed Robert's attempt to mumble. So I asked some diagnostic questions, "Where are you?"

Confused, he responded, "I don't know."

"What is your name?"

"Robert."

"Who is the president?"

"I don't know."

Just then, Dr. Carver walked into the bedroom.

Getting ready to take over, she asked, "What happened, Beth?"

"Robert had a seizure in his sleep and fell out the bed."

"Have you called 911?"

"Yes."

"How long has he been like this?"

"It lasted about 12 minutes."

"Has this happened before?"

"No."

"Did he have an injury earlier today or recently?"

"No."

"Did he hit his head when he fell?"

"I don't think so. The desk and a stack of books broke his fall."

Dr. Carver checked Robert's eyes and a few reflexes.

From the first floor, Aaron yelled, "The ambulance is here."

Two brawny emergency medical techs hurried to the bedroom and began their work by asking the same questions.

I answered their questions while looking for insurance information and phone numbers.

"Aaron, call your step-brothers and Robert's brother William. Tell them what happened and let them know we will be at Mt. Carmel Hospital."

Dr. Carter continued helping until Robert and I were in the ambulance. Then she switched roles from doctor to Kensington Carter, block captain. She gathered the boys and called and arranged for my sister Jennifer to pick up the boys at the hospital. Then Kensington dropped the boys off at the emergency room and returned home to sleep a few hours before she had to see patients herself.

* * *

Robert's sons, David and Samuel, arrived at the hospital around 6:00 am. All seemed well when the nurse announced their arrival. So, Beth saw this as an opportunity to slip out and have prayer with Frank.

"Good Morning," came Frank's rich basso profundo over the phone line.

"Frank, this is Beth. I am at the hospital with Robert. He had a seizure this morning."

"Let us pray that the Lord will heal him."

I bowed my head and waited for Frank to pray for Robert. It was understood that he would pray because I was weakened by Robert's sudden illness.

"Father God, maker of our awesome bodies, we ask that you be with Robert this morning. Keep him safe from illness and harm, Lord. Be by his bedside and protect him against the attack of our enemy…. (The prayer went on as tears streamed down my face.) May the words of our mouths and the meditations of our hearts be acceptable in thy sight, oh Lord, our Strength, and our Redeemer. This we ask in the name of the Father, Son, and Holy Ghost. Amen."

"Beth?"

"Yes?"

"Keep Julie and me informed, okay?"

"I will. Good-bye … and thanks."

As I lifted my head, David and Samuel were coming out of the treatment area. Samuel spoke as Aaron and Jason paid close attention, "Beth, we were thinking that Dad should be transferred to Memorial Hospital because all of his records are there."

"You're right. Let's make sure he is stable first before we transfer him. Aaron and Jason, I want Aunt Jenny to take you home and drive you to school. Jenny will also pick you up from school and stay at our house today and tomorrow."

* * *

School passed slowly for Aaron and Jason. At the end of the day, Jenny picked up the boys and took them home. Shortly after they were comfortable and Jenny was looking in the kitchen cabinets, the door bell rang.

"Hello, I am Jan Blumfeld. I live a few houses down. I heard that Beth was rushed to the hospital and wanted to know if I could help."

"Come in Mrs. Blumfeld, I've heard nice things about you. Unfortunately, we are meeting on an occasion such as this. I was just about to rustle up some dinner."

Mrs. Blumfield had a suggestion, "Check the freezer in the basement. Beth keeps some meals in plastic storage containers for a rainy day. There should be some stroganoff, macaroni and cheese, and bread."

"Good," said Jenny. "That will be a nice complement to the salad and potato soup I just prepared."

The phone rang. Aaron answered quickly, expecting a call from me, "Hello."

"Mom. How is Robert?"

"He is still sick, Honey. But, he will be fine. May I talk to Jenny?"

Jenny took the phone and asked, "How is Robert?"

"We are at Memorial Hospital and Robert is doing fine. He was talking and laughing when a nurse asked me to sit in the waiting room. I grew concerned because it was a while before I heard anything. So, I insisted on seeing Robert. The next thing I knew I saw him with leather wrist, foot, and chest restraints. When he saw me, he insisted that I release him. I was absolutely befuddled.

"The doctor apologized, told me that Robert had had another seizure, and had become irritated when he woke with a catheter. The doctor said they were afraid he would injure himself if he were to get up, so they placed him in restraints.

"Jenny, there was so much stress on the bed by Robert's trying to release himself that I thought it would literally come apart. He would look at me and plead for me to release him. The doctor said that he had given Robert an unusual amount of sedation, but he was not responding. In fact, he said this is highly unusual.

"Would you call Mary Mathews and let her know that I won't be able to make the group tonight. And call Kensington Carver and ask for the name of the best behavioral neurologist she knows. And, Jenny?"

"Yes."

"Can you stay the night? I don't want to leave Robert alone again."

"Sure. Just a minute, Beth.... Mrs. Blumfeld is suggesting that she can stay here with the kids while I gather a few things and bring you some soup."

"God bless you both. Thank you."

* * *

Four days later the telephone rang at the Johnson home.

"Hello, may I speak to Robert?"

"He is not here," I responded. "May I take a message?"

"This is Emanuel Sullivan. Would you ask him to return my call?"

"Manny, this is Beth. May I help?"

"Well. He hesitated. It is about his stocks."

"What about them?" I queried.

"Have you read the paper?"

"Manny, Robert is in the hospital and I have done nothing for the past four days but be by his side. I came home to shower and grab some fresh clothes for both of us. He will be home tomorrow. What is going on?"

"Your stocks took a massive plunge. I am sorry."

"How much of a massive plunge?"

No response.

"Manny, Robert is sick. Answer me."

"You've lost four-hundred-thousand dollars."

Feeling the weight of the world, I hung up the phone and staggered a few feet to the kitchen table.

* * *

The night was long without Robert next to my side. I wondered if he was okay. I wondered if anyone would hear him if he was in distress. Finally, I prayed myself to sleep.

* * *

The nurse gave Robert his discharge instructions, "Dr. Schuler has recommended Limictal 150 mg for your seizures, Mr. Johnson, to be taken twice daily. Here is your prescription. He wants to see you in his office next week. Sign these papers and you are cleared to leave."

* * *

Having Robert home was wonderful. Jason played his favorite songs on the piano, and Aaron updated him on all the sports news. We were just about to have worship when the door bell rang.

"Mrs. Blumfeld! How nice. Come in. We were just about to have worship. Join us, please."

"Thank you, Dear."

Worship was wonderful. Robert gave a short meditation and after prayer sat in the living room while Jason played hymns. Jan and I went into the kitchen to make sandwiches. She turned and looked at me apologetically, "I am so sorry, Baby. When it rains, sometimes it pours."

"What is it, Jan?"

"It's Estelle. She's gone."

"I held my mouth so Robert would not hear my scream and then fell into Jan's arms and wept."

Chapter 19 – The Last Session

Mary was outside the conference room with a half sheet cake decorated with white icing and pink and purple flowers. Written across the cake was the word "Congratulations." Admiring the cake, I reached into my bag and removed some party whistles, napkins, and eating utensils, placed them next to the cake, and poured a fresh cup of coffee. Mary's final detail was to put the finishing touches on a packet of information to present to each woman at the outset of tonight's final session.

The women began to arrive, and soon the chairs inside the conference room were filled in their usual formation. Mary was on the south side of the circle; I was on the north side. Penny sat to the right of Mary and Melanie to the right of Penny. To the left of Mary sat Felicia. Allyson was to my right, and Elisa was to the right of Allyson.

To my left sat Dorothy. All the other women with the exception of one filled up the middle. Jasmine Rivers was absent for the first time. So I opened the group with an inquiry.

Beth: "Before we get started, has anyone heard from Jasmine?"

Wilma: "I ran into her last Saturday at the Open Market. We had a nice impromptu lunch. She did not mention being absent from tonight's session."

Sue: "We had coffee last week after the session. She said nothing about missing tonight's session."

Beth: "Thank you. Okay, let's get started. I want to commend all of you for sticking with your commitment and finishing your encounter. You have accomplished a great feat! Congratulations to each of you ladies!

"Second, I want to take the time to also congratulate my co-leader Mary Mathews who has successfully defended her dissertation this past Monday. Dr. Mathews, you have our congratulations!"

The group applauded.

Beth: "Instead of taking our usual break tonight, we will stop our session a little early so that we can have some cake in celebration of our completion of the group and Dr. Mathews' completion of her program.

"Tonight we want to hear from you. We would like to hear what you think about your experiences in this group as they relate to your general group goals, which were 1) to understand aggression, 2) to understand why we treat each other badly, and 3) to explore how to teach others to treat us.

Mary: "Yes, and then you each had what we call therapeutic goals which we discussed with you individually. When these goals were set, we privately asked you to decide if you wanted to share these goals. Each of you decided to disclose your therapeutic goals to the group. Tonight if you should so choose, we are asking that you share your progress with the group. Tonight is about our progress and where do we all go from here.

"In addition to this, one of us will contact you to do a follow-up about two weeks after this last session. One year from now, Beth, who is focusing on women's issues, will do another follow-up. We just want to check on you because you have become special to us."

Beth: "Absolutely. So we will discuss the group goals as a group. Then we will take turns and discuss our personal goals. After you have presented your goal, anyone in the group may challenge you or ask questions. But, ladies, let's allow the presenter to finish first, Okay? So what do you understand about aggression?"

Penny: "Aggression is something that is found in both males and females."

Silence….

Allyson: "I challenge your statement, Penny. You have come here for 12 weeks and you are still dancing around aggression. Aggression must really be a problem for you. So, let me set the record straight. Aggression is a hostile action, directed with or without aggravation. Aggression is threatening behavior or actions. So, please stop the innocent dance. Once you said that administrators must protect their programs. Exactly what does that mean?"

Penny: "It means you do whatever you have to do to guarantee the success of your program."

Allyson: "Does that mean hurting others.-- or sabotaging the programs of others?"

Penny: "I wouldn't call it sabotaging. I think other people sabotage me. So, sometime I fight back."

Mary: "Fight?"

Penny: "Well, you know what I mean."

Mary: "I am not sure, so why don't you tell us?"

Penny: "Well, I make announcements, call in loyalties, and I delegate."

Allyson: "Do you delegate or do you throw stones and hide your hands?"

Dorothy: "So, tell us one of the worst ways you made announcements, called in loyalties or delegated."

Silence….

Penny: "Well, I…. Well, you…. This is ridiculous!"

Mary: "Ridiculous?"

Penny: "Because you don't actually expect me to tell you what I do. Do you?"

Mary: "Yes, Penny I do. We have all admitted that we have hurt other females. That is, except you. So tell us how you have hurt other females."

Silence….

With anger, Penny responded.

Penny: "Fine. I've made sure my programs were supported, not theirs. I stacked the deck. I planned trips and lowered the body count when my competition was having programs. I've called in favors. I tell weak-minded women how to think. I've suggested that if people knew what someone did, they wouldn't like them. And, I let my friends know that I expect loyalty."

Allyson: "Does lowering the body count mean distracting people so that your opponent won't have a good turn-out? Seeing someone else's disappointment must really satisfy you."

Melanie: "Penny you are awful!"

Beth: "We are not here to judge one another. There must be a reason why Penny waited so long to share this."

Penny: "I really don't call these things abuse. I call them survival."

Beth: "Where did you learn to survive like this?"

Penny: "From my mother and aunt."

Beth: "Tell us more."

Penny: "My mother would work long hours and leave my aunt in charge at our home. My aunt was three years older than I and lived with us.

"When my mother would come home from a long day's work, she wouldn't take any stuff. She expected everything to be done right: the dishes, the floors, our clothes washed and ironed for the next day. If things weren't done right, there would be a price to pay.

"My aunt was close to our age so we didn't always want to listen to her. Perhaps one of the reasons was that she used her power to make us wash her clothes and do her work, too.

"She was very smart. She wouldn't get indignant or upset when we objected or disobeyed. She would calmly say: "I will have to discuss your behavior with your mother," and we would shake in our boots.

"Once Momma started swinging, we would all get out of her way. If we should be unfortunate enough to be in the way, we would get hit.

"But, I am not an abuser. I never whipped my kids. I don't holler and shout because I do not want to be abusive. If anyone is suggesting that, let me set the record straight and say that I am not an abuser. Women just whine and complain about much of nothing."

Elisa: "You mean 'you women'? Get this... I have not spent 12 weeks 'whining and complaining about much of nothing.' I have experienced some real pain and some real healing. You have probably hurt a lot of people with your attitude about aggression.

"Listen very carefully, Penny. It appears that you think of only yourself. Consider my life. I have suffered at the hands of other women long before a husband punched me in the face. And for the first time in this group, I get that there is a fine line between being a victim and being a perpetrator.

"The women in my family unknowingly laid the foundation for my acceptance of abuse. When I met my abusive husband, the receptors for abuse were already there. I could not recognize abuse because I was taught subtle forms of abuse, which according to our society, is not really abuse. So, it became very easy for me to accept all the belittling and demeaning acts that I should have recognized as abuse in my twisted relationship with my husband.

"My mother failed me. She should have taught me these things. I had the foundation laid to become a victim by the women in my family. My father didn't bang on my mother. He was absent. Perhaps his absence was problematic in itself; but know that I experienced rejection and aggression from my mother. I did what was done to me.

"My mother was distant to me, and I was distant to my daughter. I chose distant people and cried when they were distant. I chose abusive people and cried when they were abusive.

"So, what did I do? The same thing you did. I compensated by becoming like my abusers. I learned to be distant, condescending, and not take responsibility for my actions. I have hurt people and I admit it. And, I have been hurt by people; so don't you dare sit there and suggest that the pain of aggression is not real. It's real all right. It's real whether you hit with a fist, hit with withdrawal of affection, or hit by manipulation. It's real and I have been sick from it and sick of it."

Dorothy: "Penny who are you trying to convince, us or you?"

Mary: "Penny, could it be that you have grown into a woman who admires the subtleness of your aunt and the strength of your mother?"

Penny: "I don't know. Maybe."

Silence….

Beth: "Penny, what do you think about getting hit for some past event your mother remembered that you did while she was beating one of your siblings?"

Penny: "I thought I would stay on the porch."

Beth: "Do you think that hitting someone for a past offense is rational behavior?"

Penny: "I don't know."

Beth: "So is it okay for your husband to hit you tonight for something you did or said to him six months ago?"

Penny: "Of course it isn't."

Beth: "So was it okay for your mother to hit after the fact?"

Tears began to stream down Penny's face.

Penny: "I guess not. It is hitting."

Beth: "Describe what you call beatings."

Penny: "She would use an extension cord or a belt and would hit us wherever she could. Once she grabbed a coat hanger that was unraveled, and I threw up my hands to protect my face. I still have the scars on my hand."

Beth: "Penny that was physical abuse. Your aunt abused you, too, with intimidation. Unfortunately, we are in our last session; still, I really want to speak with you after the session because we can't leave you like this. I want to recommend some follow-up for you. Some of the behaviors you described are highly subtle abuse, and some are blatant abuse.

"We learn what is taught to us. Males act out rough-and-tumble behavior early in life. As a result; some men grow up to act out rough-and-tumble behavior when showing aggression toward women. Although their behavior starts out mimicking the subtle behaviors women do, it escalates into what they have learned is acceptable behavior in men: rough contact.

"Females also learn to abuse early in life. We call their abuse relational aggression. It can be seen as early as three years of age. Please understand: the more subtle the abuse, the greater the psychological effect. So we can't excuse abuse on the grounds that it wasn't a punch to the face. Abuse is abuse no matter how subtle.

"I have worked with many women who have abused and have been abused by men. I find it interesting that many of these women did not come from homes where the father abused the mother. What they did have in common was that they watched how the females in their family treated each other. They also watched how females outside their families treated other females. It is almost as if females lay the receptors for abuse."

Allyson: "Receptors?"

Beth: "Yes, receptors. The thing one plugs another into. Elisa, may I use you for example?"

Elisa: "Yes."

Beth: "You had issues with your mother?"

Elisa: "Yes."

Beth: "Did you see your father mistreat your mother?"

Elisa: "No."

Beth: "Your daughter had issues with you, correct?"

Elisa: "Yes."

Beth: "How have you dealt with your own abuse with your daughter?"

Elisa: "I left my ex-husband when my daughter was just a toddler. I taught her not to ever tolerate abuse."

Beth: "Has your daughter been abused by her husband?"

Elisa: "Absolutely not."

Beth: "Why not?"

Elisa: "Well, probably because I was vocal about not tolerating abuse. I really did not take much from anyone after I became stronger. Then again, maybe she could see what abuse did to me. At any rate, we openly discussed abuse. The challenge to me was not to repeat the behaviors I saw my mother doing. Later on in life, my mother and I became close and we discussed abuse in the presence of my daughter. We did not treat it like a secret."

Beth: "Since we started this group, I have tried very hard not to influence your opinions about abuse and let you come to your own conclusions. However, let me say that women have more to do with the perpetuation of abuse than we think. If we are going to truly make a significant impact in domestic violence; we must teach women and children to recognize subtle violence."

Silence....

"Okay, Allyson said that aggression is real and it involves threats and hostile actions. I don't think anyone will dispute this. What we have not discussed, other than aggression being a learned behavior, is why do we treat each other badly?"

Melanie: "We know it's jealously!"

Heads nodded in agreement.

Madison: "Well, that's true, but I think that insecurity has a lot to do with it, too."

Allyson: "Don't forget control and anger."

Mary: "So, it's jealously, insecurity, control and anger?"

Bertha: "I think that we have learned how to treat women badly from watching other women. It's learned behavior. We can do stuff to each other that men just wouldn't detect. I know that I have spent time in my life dealing with my own insecurity. Sometimes I directed my anger against secure women because I was insecure.

"I have so many things going for me; yet, I put up with a lot of stuff. Maybe because I saw my mother put up with a lot of stuff from my dad. I was grown when she divorced him. And even after that, I had to spend Christmas and other holidays sitting across the table from my politely smiling mother and my father's silly flashy girlfriend, who had no doubt been his girlfriend for a long time.

"The saddest part about all of this is how I watched my mother and yet entered into the same kind of abuse. My daughter is now watching me. What am I teaching her? We have learned to do the things we do, and we have learned to accept the things we accept."

Felicia: "You don't always do the same thing; sometimes we go to the other extreme. I always saw my mother being pimped by men and I did the opposite."

Beth: "So, how should we teach others to treat us?"

Madison: "We have to teach both women and kids at the same time."

Beth: "But how do we do this?"

Sue: "Well, I guess we will have to start with teaching children to respect other children and all females. At the same time, we will have to model the correct behavior to our daughters and peers. Jasmine and I talked about this over lunch. I really don't want to teach my children that Wilma is the enemy and to hate my husband's other child. We can all coexist.

"Well, even if I should decide to stay with Preston, I want to teach my daughters to recognize abuse and to walk away from anyone who would treat them in any way other than how God intended for them to be treated. I want to teach them to set boundaries for the people in their lives and to respect themselves, not because they are all that − you know − puffed up. I want them to be confident knowing that God values them so very much. Frankly, we must teach this early in their lives."

Wilma: "I agree. Jasmine and I talked about this, too. I really don't want my child not to know his or her siblings or father. So that will probably mean keeping a low profile when my child is with Sue and Preston. So be it.

"This experience of listening to all of you – especially Jasmine, Dorothy and Felicia – has helped me understand that marriage is sacred. You know, four months ago, I would have been so happy to have what Sue had. Now, I realize that if I had Preston, he would probably cheat on me, too. Women should not fight over men. We should simply join forces and insist that they declare their intentions and make their choices. And, when they make their choices, we should hold men to them."

Sue turned toward Wilma.

Sue: "Wilma, it's going to take time to forgive you, and I don't know if I will ever trust you again. But, I will try to be fair."

Turning away from Wilma, she continued.

Sue: "You know, for me commitment is something you choose; and marriage is the by-product of that choice. Now when I contemplate our marriage; I will evaluate the level of commitment within our marriage. This is something that I have to do with Preston. And even after having a candid discussion with Preston, I have to still consider the dynamics and what they mean for me."

Mary: "How have you all met your individual goals?"

Sue: "Well, like I said. I have to work on my marriage and on me. I can be more mature and responsible. Now a part of working on this means that Wilma will have to make all her inquiries through me and not Preston. I insist that she not contact him, at least not for now."

Melanie: "I feel stronger today than I did at the beginning of the group. I understand it has been very easy for others to see my weaknesses and take advantage of them, but that was my fault. I will have to learn to limit people. A huge part of limiting people is deciding who I am and what I will tolerate. I need to work on Melanie, and not by picking up magazines and becoming other people with their skills and their lives. I need my own life."

Madison: "Wow, this has been quite an experience. For years, I have compared myself to others. I did this with my sisters and friends. I was so busy comparing that I just assumed that others were doing the same thing. My focus was on them and it should have been on me.

"Now that the group is ending, I will have to continue to take time alone and ask myself: *Who is Madison and what is her life about?* One thing I have realized is that my gifts were so different from my sisters. It would have been impossible for me to be like my sisters.

"On the other hand, I gave my future away for a few years of fame. When it was over, I felt let down by the group, when really I let myself down. I have spent years searching for that same high I received when I was performing. I came to this group thinking I was a victim, when in many ways I have been my own worst enemy.

"I am not sure what my purpose is; however, I think it has to do with working with women to help them understand their gifts and purposes. The second thing I have come to realize is that the fruit of the disobedience of the tenth commandment, 'Thou shall not covet thy neighbor's house, or his wife, or anything,' is overwhelming … is pungent.

"Coveting includes spiritual gifts also. I see coveting as the gateway to sins like adultery, false witnessing, and killing. I've come to learn that when you take your eyes off Jesus; you begin to look at what others have. The grass always looks greener on the other side. Not to mention that when you envy what someone else has, you are stepping on God's toes. God issues blessings.

"Blessings and trials, what some call crucibles, are directly related to His design on our life. I was so busy looking at others' blessings that I overlooked their trials. I would not want to go though some of the things my sisters have gone though. I was so busy looking at them that I did not develop the gifts he gave me so that I could fulfill my purpose."

Wilma: "You know, I have to take full responsibilities for my actions. I betrayed Sue and I sinned against God. I never thought about the devastation I would cause because I was concerned about my own needs and wants. Since I started participating with this group, I have had some serious conversations with my mother. I now feel especially close to her, and I am learning from some of her mistakes. I never realized how much alike we are.

"My prayer, at this point in my life, is for a healthy relationship between my child and his or her father and his father's family. I really don't want my baby to experience the pains of growing up without a father.

"Again, I apologize to you, Sue, for abusing you. I thought abuse was to physically hurt someone. Now I know that subtle abuse is also devastating."

Renée: "I have decided to choose a career and not a job and enroll in a two-year nursing program like my daughter Kennedy. This should keep me busy and keep me out of the clubs.

"Bertha brought her daughter Casey over for Nana's birthday party last week, and she and Kennedy really hit it off. My daughter asked Bertha's daughter to baby-sit once she has the baby and goes back to school. We figure that it just isn't right to give Nana someone else to raise."

Bertha: "I have decided to ask my family to join me in therapy to work on me. Hopefully, therapy will kill three birds with one stone by helping my daughter, my marriage, and me. I believe if I change, my marriage will change. If my marriage changes, then perhaps the influence it has on my daughter will be positive. I just hope that, unlike my mother, I haven't waited too late to take a stand."

Dorothy: "I had to take a serious look at my behavior and in doing that, I had to really think about my family of origin. It has really influenced the choices I have made over the years. I say 'influenced' because it laid the foundation for some of my behavior; but, ultimately the choices I made were mine and no one else's.

"I am addicted to unavailable men. Because of my father's character, I flirt with danger. I find men attractive who have a tendency toward violence. I brush everything off with humor and being sassy like my mother did. It's time for me to forgive my dad and mom and get on with my 'life according to Dorothy.'

"I reject wearing the metaphoric shoes of both my parents. It is time for Dorothy to go shoe shopping for Dorothy. I don't know what to do about my husband since he is serving a life sentence; but there is life without men. I guess I wanted unavailable men and I got just what I wanted. The irony is that while I was choosing unavailable men, I will spend the rest of my life without a man."

Felicia: "Well I can certainly identify with much of what Dorothy has said. My response to my family of origin was to do the opposite of my mother. I think if I am honest with myself, I chose to be the abuser and not the abused.

"Unfortunately, I am in a similar situation as Bertha, asking how do I undo the damage. Actually, I don't know if I can undo the damage; so I will just live each day and model a different type of behavior in the presence of my children. And if my children should decide to make the same mistakes, I will have to be patient with them. I know they will make mistakes; that is the nature of being human.

"As for the here-and-now, the men living with me will simply have to live somewhere else, and I will run my business like a business. I will talk with my baby girl and all my kids and tell them about my mistakes. That is all I can do.

"On the other hand, no it is not all I can do. I can relocate my office, too. Oh, and give myself some healing time and time to build new skills before I enter into a new relationship with a man."

Allyson: "This has been such a great experience for me. I am so glad I was able to spend the past 12 weeks with you. I have learned so much about myself and so much about life. I am sure that each of you has in some way helped me to become a better social worker and a better therapist. I know that I will be a better wife because of all the genuine things you shared.

"When I came here, my definition of abuse was 'any unreasonable measure intended to bring pain, especially in a subordinate/insubordinate relationship.' Although my definition has not changed: I now understand how subtle women are in administering abuse toward one another. You have definitely helped me become a better diagnostician."

Mary: "Unfortunately, Jasmine is not here to share with us tonight; but, we will contact her to see if she is all right. In about two weeks, you will receive follow-up calls from us just checking to see if you have followed any recommendations we have given and just to see how you are doing. Is that okay with everyone?"

Heads nodded.

Mary: "Let's take our break now and have some cake and punch. If you have any questions or concerns, Beth and I will address them at that time."

Beth: "There are exit folders on the table over there. Find the one with your name on it and you can discuss any recommendations we may have for your continued success."

***

I was concerned about Jasmine's no-show; after speaking with Penny, I called Jasmine.

Upon dialing the number I became baffled. A recorded voice announced that there was no such number in service. As I pondered what all this meant, my attention was quickly diverted to Allyson who called my name from across the room.

Allyson began with, "Beth, I want to thank you so much for this group and the focus group. They were so wonderful. Are you going to have any more groups?

Still perplexed, I answered, "Not at this time. My comprehensive examinations are scheduled for June and then I will be absorbed with writing my dissertation."

When the break was over, the women mostly talked about continuing their relationship with one another. After about 10 minutes, they said their goodbyes and left the conference room. Mary pulled Penny aside, and once again, the recommendation was made for Penny to continue with therapy as Mary handed her the names of a few therapists. Penny thanked Mary and departed, providing the opportunity for Mary and me to talk.

Mary began by asking if I were going to write my soap notes now.

"No, not tonight. I am still concerned about Robert. Listen, thank you so very much for leading out. You were fantastic. Can we have lunch or coffee Monday?"

"That sounds good."

* * *

Bretton Drive was especially lovely because of the many tulips that sprinkled the landscapes of the custom brick homes. Tulips signaled the promise of all sorts and varieties of perennials and annuals to follow. I smiled as I thought about turning in for the evening early. When I reached the house, I phoned Robert to let him know that I was rounding the corner. To my surprise, the boys had already eaten pizza for dinner, completed their homework and were preparing to watch a movie in the family room.

After climbing the stairs to the second floor, I smelled the sweet scent of Japanese Cherry Blossoms coming from the master suite. When I opened the door there were hot salmon petals sprinkles on top of bronze satin sheets. Grapes and strawberries sat in a crystal bowl with giant cashews, smoked cheese and a variety of crackers next to the fruit.

Soft music was playing against the sound of running bath water. The tub was filling up with bubbles smelling of the

Japanese Cherry Blossoms that had caught my attention originally. Candles surrounded the tub. It was a relaxing evening.

* * *

"Good Morning, Beth."

"Good Morning, Frank."

"What is on your mind this morning?"

"Frank, I am tired and I just don't know if I can do this school thing."

"What does Robert say?"

"You know Robert is always encouraging me. I will talk to him today."

"Let us pray for wisdom."

"How about you? What's on your mind?"

"I have negotiations today and I want to ask for the power of the Holy Ghost."

"Is that it?"

"Oh, pray that we not get weary of well doing. And, pray that our hearts and minds will be focused on God, especially today."

"Let's pray."

* * *

It was noon already and the morning therapy sessions went well. I couldn't help think of Jasmine Rivers. I opened my leather brief case, pulled out her contact sheets, and called the back-up numbers listed under Jasmine's name. None of the numbers were in service. This was strange. While the phone was still in my hand, I decided to call Jan Blumfeld to let her know the sessions were over.

"Hello Mrs. Blumfeld. How are you?"

"Blessed, Child, blessed."

"I wanted you to know that we completed the final group last evening and to thank you so very much for helping with the cooking and with the fellows."

"What is the next thing on your program?"

"Well, I take my comprehensives in June and there is writing after that. But…."

"Yes."

"I am so very tired, I just don't know if I can do this. Besides, it takes so much time away from Robert and the boys."

"Beth, they are fine and I will help you. Hush that talk."

"Seriously, Robert is not doing well and I am needed at home."

"Beth, you are talking about writing and staying home for a year. Will you stop by my house on your way home from work today?"

"I don't mean to be rude or ungrateful; but, Fridays are really busy for me, Jan. Will, it take long?"

"Not at all."

"Okay, I will see you just before 4 o'clock."

* * *

Jan opened the heavy red door and led me to the study. She placed a step-stool on the floor in front of the built-in book shelves. "There." She slid out an ornate box made of red silk fabric and heavy-beaded ribbon. "This is for you."

"For me, whatever is it?"

"Let's go into the dining room. Shall we?"

She led me to the dining room table.

I selected the chair next to the head chair; then slowly pulled out the chair and proceeded to sit down even more slowly.

"Dear, I have failed to tell you the extent of my relationship with Estelle Devereaux. When I was in the hospital, we visited each other and shared some secrets. She told me all about you and how fondly she felt toward you. When she went home, we kept up our relationship and she monitored your progress through me. She was so proud of the work you were doing on women and abuse that she asked me to encourage you when she was gone. She asked me to give this to you at just the right time and I believe the right time is right now. I believe if you would open this box, you would find some of her deepest feelings. Not finishing this work is not an option: you must finish. She rested on the fact that someone would make a difference for women experiencing the pain she was so frightened of.

"Standing, Jan continued… "Well, dear, you must have plenty to do."

"Thank you, Jan. Once again I feel selfishly silly."

* * *

Robert was edging the lawn when I approached him carrying the box.

"Oh, I see you have your box."

"Oh my goodness! Robert, you knew?"

Chapter 20 – The Findings

I took the box to the chaise in my prayer-room and opened it. I found one pink parchment envelope. On the center of the envelope was written my name *"Elizabeth Johnson – Open this envelope first."* Under the envelope were four books, each book held closed by a pink ribbon. The letter read:

Dear Beth,

You have given me much love and I sincerely appreciate your stepping-up to the plate and becoming a daughter to me. I want to make sure you complete the work that God has started in you. So, I decided that you are to have my personal memoirs, which are contained in this box. One book contains real life events. One book contains my prayers and supplications. One book contains lessons I have been taught by wise people. The last book contains monologues to my angel, whom I have affectionately named Jasmine Rivers.

I have tied a ribbon around each journal and ask that you open the journals only after you have successfully defended your dissertation. Although my earthly possessions have been divided, what I leave you with is most valuable to me because it reflects my heart and soul through my penned thoughts.

Until we meet in Heaven,

Estelle

I thought about what it would be like to introduce my mother and Estelle to each other in heaven and became overwhelmed. When I looked up, Robert was standing over me saying, "Promise me you will finish." I threw my arms around him and cried a silent cry of surrender.

* * *

They say time flies when you are having fun. I felt like I had been on a rocket ship for a year.

After a lot of hard work and support from my family, I was entering the homeward stretch. I could hardly believe we were as busy as beavers making preparations for a dress rehearsal to defend my dissertation. I was glad I could count on my husband and the boys.

Since many hands make light work, I took full advantage of my supporting cast: "Robert, can you get the water from the freezer and place the water glasses at the six seats at the table?

"Dr. Warren, here are the packages of chapter 5. Can you place one at each place setting?

"Jason, I left a tray of cookies on the back seat of the car. Will you be a dear and get them and place them in the middle of the table?

"Aaron, is the PowerPoint ready?

"Oh my, why am I so nervous? It's just a mock defense. What will I do next week when I have the real defense? Huh?

"Okay, Dr. Warren. Tell me who is coming."

"We have Dr. Harris, a statistician. He will be questioning you on your design, research methods, and statistical tests. Dr. Fleming is a psychologist. She will question you on the psychological soundness of your study and its implications.

Dr. Jenkins is a professor of leadership. He will question you on content and future implications. Dr. Chin is a doctor of educational leadership. She will question you about developmental indications as related to young boys and girls. And Dr. Mathews, an associate of yours, is a sociologist who will ask general questions and monitor your objectivity."

"How can I ever thank you for this?"

"We are all Christians and we have a very unique ministry. I am sure you will understand it as time goes by. Sometime in the future we will ask you to help someone else go through the same process. Be ready to help."

The door bell rang and Dr. Mary Mathews arrived, followed by Dr. Fleming and the others. Soon the scholarly team and I were all seated in the dining room. Robert, the boys, and Mrs. Blumfeld sat in the adjacent breakfast nook listening intently. Once they were all seated at the table, Dr. Warren began.

"I would like to thank you for agreeing to come out tonight to question Beth Johnson on her scholarly work. We are trying to create a replica of her impending dissertation defense. So, Beth will give a 20 minute presentation about her work.

"At the end of 20 minutes, she will be seated and we will begin three rounds of questions. The first round will serve as a warm-up to further familiarize ourselves with her study and to ask obvious questions. In the second round, more intense questions will be asked. You will focus on your area of expertise and you may be as brutal as you choose. In the third round, you will focus on future implications as they relate to your or any other person's discipline.

"After she completes the third round, she will be excused and we will deliberate just as her committee will deliberate next week. After the deliberation, she will join us again and we will tell her if she would have passed or not. Then we will give her pointers on how to prepare for her defense next week. Are there any questions?"

Pause....

"Beth, you may present."

The presentation lasted 18 minutes and round one began, lasting thirty minutes. This was followed by round two.

Round two lasted fifty-five minutes, followed by round three, lasting forty minutes.

After over two hours of grueling questions, Dr. Warren invited me to leave the room. Robert, Mrs. Blumfeld, the boys, and I went downstairs and waited. After thirty minutes, I was summoned. Robert, Mrs. Blumfeld, and the boys crowded on the stairs to listen with bated breath.

It wasn't until Dr. Warren exclaimed, "Congratulations," that I was able to exhale in relief. I hugged Dr. Warren. Then I shook the hand of each participant and offered them some of Mrs. Blumfeld's home-made soup and bread. They graciously declined, gave me some tips, and were off as quickly as they had come.

Robert smiled and wrapped his long arms around me. One by one, Aaron, Jason and Mrs. Blumfeld offered their embraces. Then Mrs. Blumfeld stirred the large pot of soup simmering on the stove, saying, "I do believe it is time for soup."

As we sat around the table, Aaron asked me to explain the study.

"Do you really want to know? Well, let's see if I can summarize." Picking up three pieces of paper from the fax machine, I began, "Okay, I am going to give you each a piece of paper."

On the first sheet of paper, I wrote: "What acts or behaviors conducted by women do women perceive as abuse or mistreatment?" and gave it to Aaron.

On the second sheet, I wrote: "Are these perceptions of abuse/mistreatment related to a gender profile?" and gave it to Jason.

On the third sheet of paper, I wrote: "What is the relationship between a woman's personal experience as both victim and perpetrator of abuse and race, age, and education?" and gave it to Mrs. Blumfeld.

I asked Aaron to read his question. "What acts or behaviors conducted by women do women perceive as abuse or mistreatment?"

I answered, "Items on the overt behavior scale were consistently considered abusive when performed by one woman on another, regardless of race or age. These overt actions included,

- Manipulating easy-going women,
- Sleeping with another woman's husband,
- Sleeping with another woman's husband to hurt her,
- Gossiping to ruin her reputation,

- Betraying her,
- Humiliating her,
- Giving her hurtful messages,
- Destroying her self-esteem,
- Destroying her work, and
- Yelling at her.

Items on the covert behavior scale were not considered abusive when conducted by one woman on another. Covert included,

- Refusing to acknowledge her presence,
- Giving her unsolicited opinions,
- Disliking her for being confident,
- Keeping her at a distance,
- Ignoring her because of her appearance,
- Not associating with her because of social status,
- Withdrawing affection from her,
- Failing to support her efforts,
- Avoiding her because of her friends, and
- Interfering with her spiritual growth.

"One interesting finding concerning your question, Aaron, is that Caucasian women and older women were more likely to recognize abuse.

"Now Jason, read your question."

Jason complied, "Are these perceptions of abuse or mistreatment related to gender self-concept?"

"The answer to your question is that it did not matter how feminine or masculine the woman, they felt the same way about abuse.

"Now, Mrs. Blumfeld, read your question."

Mrs. Blumfeld read, "What is the relationship between a woman's personal experience as both victim and perpetrator of abuse and her race, age, and education?"

I answered that question clearly, "By a large margin, women who reported being abused more possessed one of three distinct characteristics. They

- were Caucasian/White,
- were between the ages of 40 and 49, and
- had graduate degrees.

"By contrast, the majority of women who reported being abused least also posessed one of three distinct characteristics. They

- were African American,
- were between the ages of 18 and 20, and
- had high school diplomas or certificates of high-school completion.

On the other hand, there was no significant relationship or pattern between the perceived perpetrators' age, race, and educational level. Interestingly, there is also no pattern for men who abuse women.

This brings to mind Frederick Douglass' assertion that prejudice defies conventional wisdom in that it has nothing to do with race or color. Its motives and mainstream are from another source [The Color Line].

The simple fact that researchers have a difficult time profiling abusers makes me think that abuse, too, is from another source. We cannot say an abuser is old or young, rich or poor, educated or non-educated, or is a member of a certain ethnic group. I believe that what Douglass and I are both referring to is a demonic source.

Now let me list some of the other findings.

- 75-95 percent of women in the study recognized when behaviors were abusive acts between women.
- Over 60 percent of subjects reported having been abused.
- 35 percent of subjects reported abusing other women.
- Women reporting they had been abused perceived overt acts as abusive.
- Women reporting abusing other women say they do so by covert and overt behaviors.
- Women model behavior to their children.
- Children learn aggression from both parents.
- Around the age of 8, girls are taught to use sophisticated forms of communication that are less forthright and discerning of their true feelings.
- Girls become more skilled at hidden meaning and meanness as they get older.
- Women perceive more abuse as they get older.
- Aggression, or abuse, learned early becomes a part of the psychological foundation of girls which, ironically, enables them to accept abuse later in life.
- Jealously, anger, insecurity and control were cited as reasons for abuse among women.
- More subjects report being abused by women than by men.
- African American women report receiving abuse from and abusing other women less than subjects of other racial groups.

The desensitization of abuse among African American women is attributed to slavery. It is thought that African American women have grown accustomed to harsh treatment and are more accepting of negative behavior.

Jason looked with amazement, saying: "Mom, I did not think your dissertation would be all that. You are going to do just fine."

As Jason finished his welcome encouragement, loud, rumbling thunder sounded. A bright flash of lightening pierced the sky. Could this be an electrical storm? Where did it come from? So we wondered!

Commander Warmouth was flying over our home and decided to check on my progress. Appalled, he shouted and his form jerked with trembling anger. My angel was joined by another in protecting the home and its inhabitants.

Warmouth, jetted back to his command post, summoning his soldiers, "How could you be so preposterously inferior, you pathetic idiots? I gave you one simple task and you failed miserably. Do you realize the magnitude of this, you imbeciles!

"Don't you know we specialize in capturing the worrisome little worms before they are seven years of age? Now, we run the risk of these pathetic beings uncovering our strategies. They will attempt to teach more effective communication skills and self awareness to their worms.

"We teach children, the worms that they are, to mask emotional conflict. We want to get them young so we can manipulate their characters. And, if we have their characters, we have them for life! Don't you get it: we want aggression and violence embedded into their characters! This failure could mean a serious assault on one of our most powerful weapon.

"How do you think we are so successful at domestic violence? We teach it through women. We use the tongues of women! We use their behavior! We use them to actively teach or passively model the acceptance of violence."

"We also benefit when churches lose members because of the behavior of women. There are more women than men. They abuse more than men; and women are more aware of emotions; so they are our best tools. Why do you think our divisions are named emotions? We thrive on the comparativeness and competition of women. It evokes emotions! That's how we get into them, emotions."

"Their stress and distrust of each other keep their subculture fixed and provide a cause for business as usual in society. Satan forbid, we should have harmony among women. It would change the world. Churches would grow. And before you know it; we will see…I can't even say the name…in the clouds returning.

"HAVE YOU LOST YOUR MINDS!

"Okus and Bentler, you are demoted. I will assign someone more competent to save my promotion and to decrease our burning time."

* * *

Pssst. One week later holy angels escorted my family and me to the dissertation defense. The defense was successful. One month later, I experienced the joy of graduation. But was graduation all that I had thought it would be? I looked forward to not rushing off to class or not experiencing the eye-strain of computer fatigue syndrome as I made revisions to my work. But, what I wanted most was to sleep in, in the morning.

Chapter 21 – The Dedication

Sleeping in was wonderful. Shortly after waking, I experienced conflicting emotions. So, I paused to investigate what I was feeling. After moments of complete silence, I understood that the first emotion was a sense of accomplishment and blessings. Accomplishment because I absolutely knew that God led me over the past two years as surely as he led his children in the past. Yet, to my surprise, I also felt a second emotion, a sense of loss.

Pausing to examine these emotions, I soon realized that the absence of my mother and Estelle somehow lessened the celebration of the day before. How wonderful would it have been to look upon their smiling faces, to hold them in my arms and say "Thank you."

However, if I were completely honest with myself, I would have to admit that the other conflicting emotion was another type of loss. The loss of goals to direct my behaviors and the perplexity of what to do now pained me. Putting existential questioning aside, it was much easier to simply get a cup of tea and refreshments and relax. The sane thing to do, I decided, was to take some time to luxuriate in all the personal time that had been freed up now that I had completed a major milestone. Perhaps some delectables, a lavender bath, and some chocolates would be just the ticket to reward and refresh myself before pursuing new goals in my usual Type-A manner.

So, I slipped into my long white robe and took tea and a bammy patty into the living room to the same large red sofa that Estelle and I had sat on for our very first heart-to-heart chat. On the glass table was a copy of my dissertation along side *the box*. With one cleansing exhalation, I picked up the dissertation and with relief read its dedication:

To my husband who has made all my dreams come true....
To my mother, Emma, who was my very best friend....
To Estelle Deveraux who once said to me, "I am more afraid of those
   women than the cancer that is within my body."

After reflecting on the sentiments behind the dedication, I
turned to the abstract and read:

Title: The Phenomenon of Woman-on-Woman Abuse and its
   Relationship to Gender Profile and Personal Experiences of
   Women

Name of Researcher: Elizabeth Johnson
Name and Degree of Faculty Chair: Judith Lipscomb, Ph.D.
Date Completed: July 2003

Purpose of the Study: Female-on-female aggression is often inferred, or
   drawn from studies conducted with children or males. Little or no
   information is available that reports behaviors perceived as
   mistreatment or abuse among women. The purposes of this study
   were to investigate (a) behaviors demonstrated by women that
   women consider abuse or mistreatment; (b) the extent to which
   these perceptions of abuse/ mistreatment were related to gender
   profiles; and (c) the extent to which personal experiences as
   victims or perpetrators of abuse were related to age, race, and
   education.

Method: This study used the survey research method in which
   questionnaires were mailed and self-administered to a convenience
   sample of 1,700 Mary Kay™ personnel and their associates. Six
   hundred and twenty-six of the 640 respondents who chose to
   participate in this study were included for final data analysis. The
   questionnaire was designed to elicit demographic characteristics,
   gender profile, and overt and covert acts or behaviors that may be
   considered mistreatment/abuse.

Results: Thirty-five percent of the women admitted to being perpetrators of abuse, while 59 percent reported being victims of abuse by other women. Only overt behaviors such as "sleeping with her husband to hurt her" were considered acts of abuse. Caucasians tended to view these overt acts as more abusive than other racial groups. Women in the 40-49 age range perceived these acts to be more abusive. Perceptions of abuse were not related to gender profile. In addition, women with college degrees perceived abuse more than women with high school diplomas or certificates of completion.

Conclusion

The phenomenon of Woman-on-Woman Abuse is quite real. The pain of the women in the groups confirmed that it was real. The data proved that it was real. But was that good enough? Sinking into the large red sofa, I thought of my first meeting with Estelle, sitting in my living room getting acquainted, talking of Jamaican food like bammy. Not only had I come to love bammy myself, I had also come to understand that, like the Cassava root, some of the women at the *Temple in the Sky* were sweet; and some were bitterly poisonous.

Although finished with my dissertation, I found that I only had more questions. Namely, what could be done to help heal the hurts of women who have been wounded by other women? How could I use my research to seriously impact domestic violence? And, what could be done to expose the army of darkness?

It occurred to me that perhaps there would be more guidance in *the box*. Leaning forward, placing one hand on the lid of the box, I reached in and removed the four journals from the box. Pulling open one pink ribbon, I opened the book which was titled: *Prayers and Supplications*. A tear traced down my face as I read the first heart-wrenching prayer in the book. Anxious, I pulled another ribbon which bound another book titled: *Wisdom from Others*. Turning the page, I read a one-page worship thought about "The Girl Who Wanted a Family."

I pulled another ribbon from the third book *The Truth Is Stranger Than Fiction – Real Life Events*. The book opened to a page marked with a salmon colored rose. On the top of the page was the title "Beth and I Have Traveled Similar Roads." Overcome by its contents, I struggled to open the final book. Lastly, I pulled the fourth ribbon from the last book entitled: *Conversations With My Angel, Jasmine Rivers*.

Immediately, I turned to the final chapter: "Meet Me in Heaven," and began to read. From the first page I positively knew that all my trials, all my tribulations, all the negative experiences I had had with women, all the experiences that had been shared with me by other women, including Estelle's input into my life – had happened so that God could be glorified. In that moment, I embraced the peace of knowing that in all things, God is working for the good of them who love Him and who are called according to His purpose [NIV].